THE TRANSITION

- From one hell to another -

Written by Lamont Carey

Edited by
Melanee Woodard
Miranda Sherill
Jerline Whitley

Book design and graphics created by J. P.
Lago

Vol. 3 THE TRANSITION

Copyright © 2018 by Lamont Carey

Twitter: @lamontcarey

Facebook: LaCareyentertainment,llc/ lamontcarey

Distributed Worldwide
ISBN-13: 978-1-945806-02-5

Special Thanks

Special thanks to Pharaoh, Melanee Woodard, Libra, Robert Carey, Lady Flava, Holli Holliday, Michelle Parker, Fat Dukes, Ella Carey, David Bost, Lisa Lindsey, Jacqueline Boles, Jermaine Ingram, Horace Ellis, Fred Chandler, Meryl Ironson, Joshua, Elijah, Queen Afi, Hermond Palmer, Tyrone Hicks, Shea Harris, Christine Graham, Genine Hagar, Amy Beckford, Brenda Richardson, Sherry Washington, Mira Sherill, Sharon Coker, Heather E. Strachan, Gregory Smith, Charles Mitchell, Dyone Mitchell, Tom Brown, Allie Bird, Bro. Rob, The Gilkey's, Bianca Brown, my family, my social media network family, my supporters, and any and every one that I failed to mention.

CHAPTER 1

It is completely quiet on the tier in solitary confinement except for an obese white correctional officer doing his rounds. As he stops at each cell, all you can hear is his shoes clicking against the shiny floor, the slight squeak of his belly rotating over his belt and the rustle of fabric rubbing as he walks. He quickly removes his cap and sighs before running his hand through his short blonde hair to allow some air to cool his head. He then slowly tugs the cap down onto his head before unlocking the next window slab.

"Mr. Ford.... You'll be released from solitary confinement and prison around 6am.

Congratulations. You'll be done with this place. I hope for good."

Sherman is laid back on his bunk with his hands underneath his head. He was staring at the ceiling until the guard got his attention. Now he stares at the window slit. All he can see is the tier light framing the guard's chubby face.

"Yea. Thanks." Sherman says, emotionless.

"You don't sound too excited." The guard replies, slightly out of breath.

"I've been here before and didn't make it out." Sherman says with the same emotion as he displayed before.

The guard chuckled. "I don't mean to laugh but, this may humor you. They'll be a team of us escorting you out in the morning. You'll make it out this time. Now, I don't know what your future holds but, you'll get your freedom in the morning." The guard says as he continues to chuckle.

"Thanks," Sherman says as he directs his attention back to the ceiling.

CHAPTER 2

A black Mercedes Benz is parked in front of the Anacostia Recreation Center in Washington, DC. The park is pitch black except for the dim streetlights on the narrow road next to the Potomac River. There is new development taking place on the opposite side of the river.

Butch barely notices that the clock on the dashboard reads 1:00 am. He's alert but consumed with his own thoughts.

"Dat's what gentrification looks like," Quality says with his Dominican-mixed-with-New York City accent. He's been supplying local drug dealers with a kilogram of cocaine or less for the last two years. He smiles a lot but he's not flashy.

He wears sweat suits, a gold herringbone necklace and a submarine Rolex watch.

Butch doesn't respond.

"That's why I'm glad we got introduced. I need a strong dude in my corner. You basically did five years for killing a cop.

The streets loving dat. Plus you know how to get money. We gone get mad money together, B. We gone get so much money that your anemic ass is going to stay hot!" Quality says, jokingly as he gestures towards Butch's gloved hand on the steering wheel.

He is wearing a black jacket with the collar up and his hat pulled down to his forehead. Butch smirks and Quality giggles.

"I'm nobody's muscle. I don't live like that." Butch replies, firmly.

"That ain't what I'm saying, B. As long as the streets know you'll put that work in, they'll let you eat in peace and dats all we want is to eat in peace. You don't eva have to touch a gun as long as you with me. I need you to help me move grams. These other cats shysty. Day don't think. They rather rob me and get short money versus gettin with me and gettin rich. New York cats the same but we smarter, B. But we gone get money a long time. Da good thing about us is you know the cats that I don't know. Plus, you don't know none of the cats I fuck wit. So we keep'em off balance. You feel me? My dudes see you and be shook. We drop your name because it's ringing about the cop killing. They scared straight on my end because they think you on murder time. They stay in line.

9

Your dudes see you got work and they come to you. Double respect. They know you get money and bodies. Plus I wanna fade to black and allow you to get your shine. You feel me, B?" Quality says.

Butch nods his head. "Yea. I need to shoot some shit to my man behind the wall," Butch replies.

"I heard it was mad money down there, B. Now you know they closing that Lorton spot down. They been shipping dudes all over the country. So I'm not sure if we can depend on that as a long term investment, B." Quality says.

"We can get that money until they ship my man and dem." Butch replies.

"Cool, B. That's your little side hustle. Ain't enough money in that for me unless we were in there. Then we could sell the shit ten times the price but it ain't worth the risk for me. I hope you change your mind because we don't need that short money. I know you tryna look out for your homies and dem so I'ma chill. You just have to keep some distance between us and dat. You feel me, B?"

Butch nods his head in agreement.

"It's time for you to take it nice and easy. You been through a lifetime and you're only 20, B. Let's get this money and go live high on a hill!" Quality continued.

A van is driving down the dark road. It stops a few yards from them.

"Showtime. Flash the lights." Quality says. After Butch complies, the van stops

40 feet away from them. Quality grabs a book bag off the backseat and smiles, "Let me go grab these twenty bricks." He says as he exits the vehicle.

The passenger exits the van and smiles at Quality as he walks in between the two vehicles. He starts digging into the book bag.

Butch slams on the gas and rams Quality's body. His body slips underneath the left tire and the back tire rolls over his lower legs, crushing them. He then rams the passenger, pinning him in-between the car and truck. As his body collapses onto the hood, the driver riddles the front of the car with a Mac-10 uzi. Butch crouches down and leans his head toward the steering wheel as he opens the car door.

The flashing lights of four Park Police cruisers immediately invades the darkness from the back of the building with their sirens and tires screaming. Butch exits the car in a crouched position and starts shooting at the driver while glancing back and forth. He shoots the driver in the neck. The driver grabs his neck and slumps over. Butch fires at the cop's cars as they skid to a halt and duck for cover. He spots the book bag and grabs it just as the cops peel out of their cars. Butch fires at the cars. The bag drops out of his hand and bundles of money tumble onto the asphalt. As some of the officers return fire, he quickly snatches a few bundles of money. He backs up and continues to shoot at the cops, while dashing around the back of the recreation center, past the fenced-in public swimming pool. Some of the cops cautiously follow, while another one jumps in his car to pursue him. Butch runs onto the bridge behind the recreation center heading toward Anacostia High School, across from a residential area. Sirens can be heard in the distance as he runs down an alleyway and hides in the trunk of an abandoned car. The sirens and flashing lights awaken the community as they swarm the residential area.

CHAPTER 3

Charlie guides his mop bucket with the mop stick. The squeaking wheels invade the quiet housing unit. The unit is wall to wall white and extremely clean. He waves to an unseen guard behind him as he makes his way to the stairs. No other human is in-sight. There are two floors with a common area that is above the bottom floor. It has an octagonal shape. There are four flat screen TVs spaced out at different angles on the wall. Metal circular tables are positioned in different locations near the TVs. The first floor cells can be seen from the common area. The first and second floor has thirty cells on each side of the tier that line the wall around the shape of the common area.

The cell at the top of the stairs buzzes as it is electronically unlocked. The mop bucket clangs against each step as Charlie drags it up the staircase to the second floor. He is a slender man with shaggy dark brown hair and a matching mustache. He stops at cell 32, peers in, and sees the two men sound asleep on their bunk beds. He scans around the room at the small metal table opposite the bunk beds. Attached to the bottom bed are two drawers. The combination sink-and-toilet is near the door. From where he is standing, he can only see the tip of the toilet seat. He taps on the plexiglass of the narrow window on the door.

"Aryyyyyyyanssssssss. Sorry to disturb you gentlemen but is it possible that an old country boy like me could come in?"

Charlie says with his thick Mississippi accent before opening the door.

Brace watches from cell 30 on the bottom floor as Charlie enters the cell leaving his mop bucket near the door.

One of the huge white men sits up on the edge of the bottom bunk, flashing the "White Power" sign to Charlie. He is shirtless and wearing only his boxers. His hand ruffles through his short blonde hair before wiping around his green eyes. The man on the top bunk irritably pulls himself into a seated position and rubs his eyes. He is hairless with huge tattoos scattered around his upper-body and head.

"What's going on, guys? Come on. Come on." Charlie says clapping his hands. "You fuckin' guys are pitiful? What if I was one of those niggers or spicks or anybody else for Christ's sake? You fuckin' nitwits would be slaughtered like sheep. When the door buzzes, you fuckers get on up! Not just get up, you fuckers be prepared to defend yo fuckin selves. I should mop this damn room with the likes of you both. You fucks. Good thing I am not your fucking enemy." Charlie shakes his head and his hair swings against his face as he stands with clenched fist.

"We're sorry, Charlie. We wasn't expecting you." Decker says from his seated position on the bottom bunk.

Charlie swiftly kicks the leg of the bottom bunk. "Dat's da freaking point, you fucks! I repeat: door opens, asses up and ready to be attacked. I'ma try dis again. Lie ya asses down." Charlie barks.

"Are you serious?" Bobby says from the top bunk.

Charlie stares him directly in his eyes and walks out of the door. The men lie back down. Charlie makes a buzzing sound and snatches the door open. Both men leap up into a seated position with their feet off the bed. Bobby's feet almost hit Decker in the face. Charlie claps. "That's more fuckin' like it. Ya see. Like dis, ya have a chance to defend yaself. I need ya to train yo fucking minds to say, door buzzard means war." Charlie says. "You never know when it's coming so you have to always be fuckin' prepared for it," he sighs. "Now...I can get to why I came'ere." Charlie sighs again, "Decker, do ya have some gifts for me from the metal shop?"

Decker immediately reaches into his drawer beneath the bed. "Yea, I made 13 knives - not shanks – with solid handles. I have 27 more to go. I should be done by the middle of next week." He says as he turns to Charlie with the knives wrapped in an old oily shirt.

"Put dem in the bucket for me." Charlie says as he directs his attention to Bobby. "Bobby, get down for a minute. I wanna talk to ya." Charlies says as Decker politely moves pass him into the hallway where he places the knives into the dirty mop water, after he closed the door behind him. Bobby obediently gets off of the bed.

"Ya know I had you working right along-
side me on the compound. You didn't
pick up that I am a very fragile but
committed country boy from the sticks of
Mississippi? And the one ding about us
is we po, we racist, we loyal, and we kin.
I thought you were my kin." Charlie says
with a look of despair.

Bobby backs into the wall as his
face goes white and his eyes widen with
a look of shock. "Brother, you just broke
my heart. You doubting my loyalty? I
killed three niggers and two spicks for
you. For the Brotherhood."

"Dats true...but, I think that's where you
started thinkin fo' yo self. Ya got an idea
in your fat fuckin head where you could
be me? I don't know why ya wanna be
me.

There is nothing pretty about who I am or what I do for the Brotherhood...but I got natural life in here. So all I got is fo'eva and my position in the Brotherhood. Now you want to overthrow what I have and just leave me with natural life. Do ya know how fuckin depressing it is to just have natural life to look fo'? " Charlie says shaking his head in disbelief.

"I swear I don't have no idea what you talking about?" Bobby pleads.

Charlie steps nose to nose with him and stares insanely into his eyes. "You really think Old Chuck fell off the back of a pick-up and been knocked senseless? The one thing I hate more than a rat, more than a backstabber and more than a liar is a lying ass coward. Pull yo britches up. You been trapped. Can't you feel your eyes-wide like a deer in headlights? I gots you in my scope. Talk coward or I'ma gut you right here. Right now." Charlie says with an eerie calmness.

"I heard some of those stories about what I said. It ain't true. I was trying to get the Brothers to be more confident and more committed to controlling the filth we have to share air with and to increase our profits." Bobby replies.

"So, you don't think they're committed or making enough money?" Charlie replies.

"Some of them aren't really true Aryans. They're not understanding why we're superior and why we have to be in control." Bobby replies.

"And the money?" Charlie questions.

"Some were saying, we don't share in the profits and I told them if they increase production and distribution, their profits would increase." Bobby says, reassuringly.

"Ya sound like a leader to me." Charlie says smiling.

"Noooooo. I thought I was reinforcing your messaging." Bobby says.

Charlie backs up and smiles. "Now I wouldn't say it so eloquently like you just did. Shit. I woke ya up for nothing."

Bobby starts smiling. Charlie turns and walks to the doorway. Bobby sighs.

"Decker, get on in here. I woke ya up for nothin'." Charlie says humorously. He pats Decker on his back with three spaced fingers as he exits the room.

Bobby sighs and climbs up on his bunk and pulls his sheet up to his neck.

"That was something. I'll tell you about it in the morning." Bobby says as he rolls over to face the wall.

Decker grabs his knife from under his pillow and swiftly stands up on the edge of his bed. He presses his body weight on Bobby's head and repeatedly stabs him to death.

CHAPTER 4

With eyes that match his name, Blue Eyes is staring silently through the passenger window of the U.S. Marshal's Prisoner Transport Bus. He has experienced horrors that no 19-year-old should ever witness.

There are twelve large 737 air-crafts positioned around the runway. Over 400 prisoners in brown slacks and shirts are being marched from thirteen prison buses onto the air-crafts by armed U.S. Marshals. The prisoners scuttle along in single file lines with a chain connecting their shackles and handcuffs together.

Rakeys nudges him with his shoulder. Blue Eyes looks over at his older companion. "Looks like a damn shipment of niggers on their way to their new plantation." Rakeys says with disappointment. He clenches his fists and his lean muscles ripple.

Blue Eyes nods toward one plane. "It's not all us, Cuzzo. Look at all those crackers getting on that plane over there."

"Damn. Those some big ass white boys. They must be headed to Crackerville. I bet you those mutherfuckers used to fuck farm animals. Look at that nigga over there with those toddler arms. He can't even clap."

They start laughing as Rakeys mimics that man clapping. Immediately, on the tarmac, a huge white man that's chained to other white men, briskly scuttles over to a group of black prisoners and slams his forehead into the face of a black prisoner in the middle of the group. The man falls forward pulling the others chained to him down to the ground. The whites start kicking all of them. All the prisoners on Blue Eyes' bus leaps up and anxiously look toward the window. The white men are cheering and the blacks are enraged. Blue Eyes and Rakeys stand and begin assessing their threats.

Some of the U.S. Marshals on the tarmac immediately started shooting the fighting prisoners dead. The wounded men and all of the others lie down on the tarmac. The marshals wave their weapons toward them and this intensifies the rage of the prisoners on Blue Eyes' bus. Automatically, the two marshals on their bus, cock and aim their shotguns at the men. "You have two seconds to sit your asses down and shut up or I'm going to take this as an attempt to escape! One!" A marshal with a Texan voice screams. The men quickly sit. "Now bury your faces in your lap!" He bellows as he gestures with his eyes.

The prisoners do as they are told. Rakeys glances back and notices that majority of the other 38 prisoners on the bus are Caucasian. Psycho is seated in the middle row. He is a tall, muscular and bald-headed Caucasian man in his forties with tattoos all over his body. Six teardrop tattoos fall from the corner of his left eye, and three fall from his right eye. In between his eyebrows is a tattoo that reads 666. "Be prepared for anarchy. Our enemies await us." He says without looking at Skip seated next to him.

Skip is a slim Caucasian man in his twenties with five Aryan Brotherhood tattoos on his face and two teardrops dangling from the corner of his left eye. His eyebrows are shaved and the word "White" over one eye and "Power" over the other. His eyes have a mixture of determination and fear.

The teardrops are an indicator of how many men they have killed. Their victims are all black. Skip glances at Psycho. "That's a terrible thang that just happened to our Brothers."

"This is our war. These niggers and spicks don't deserve our air. We have to make sacrifices for the Aryan race. A small amount of our blood for the elimination of them... is worth the death of a few of us." Psycho replies.

Sirens can be heard loudly arriving on the scene.

Big Moe is an overbearing dark-skinned man. He's terrified. He keeps glancing up at the top of the seat in front of him. He exhales deep breaths. He looks at Black Smoke seated next to him and Black Smoke doesn't look happy, as he stares at his knees.

"How they going to just do this? I ain't sign nothing saying I'm willing to get on a plane. Fuck dis. They can't make me." Big Moe says in a complete panic.

Black Smoke shakes his head in disappointment at Big Moe as he glances across the aisle at Dre and Marc. Marc shakes his head.

"Fuck. I gotta shit." Big Moe says with a look of panic.

CHAPTER 5

Butch is asleep on the couch fully clothed with the exception of his shoes. His aunt uses her walker to slowly move over to him. Her pink nightgown doesn't lighten her anger. "Get up! Get your damn behind up! Get up, Butch! Get up now." She bellows. "I'm tired of this! It's 10 in the morning! You're just lying around here like you got it made. I've been taking care of you every since you got out that damn prison. I don't know what happened to you in there!"

"Huh? What you talking about?" He says half asleep.

"Look at you. A whole year, I can under-stand, you can't find a job. You never had one, but you you always took care of yourself every since you moved in with me, after your momma died."

"Auntie, I do help out around the house." He says cautiously.

"When was the last time you paid a bill? But you warm and comfortable, ain-t'cha? When was the last time you bought food? But your ass will eat as soon as you wake up. Fuck helping out around the house. Help me pay a bill. As a matter of fact, help me get the house back you made me lose!"

"How I make you lose your house?" He says with shame.

"You shot a cop and your ass went to jail." She barks.

"So it's my fault you lost your house because I went to jail?" He pleads.

"You damn right! You were helping pay
my mortgage! You know I was on dis-
ability and couldn't work. You so busy
trying to prove you're a big man and
shoot a damn cop. How dumb could you
be? You had responsibilities. You were
helping me! And I took care of you before you could take care of yourself."
She barks.

"Auntie, I was helping you with drug
money." He pleads.

"You didn't have a job. You had to survive somehow. You were doing great at
that. You were always successful at that.
Look at you now! How do you feel about
yourself? Tell me?" She screams.

He sits up and he wipes his eyes. Then he grabs the bundles of money underneath him and gives her a bundle and a half. "That's $15,000 dollars. I guess that will help you get back into a house." He says with disappointment. "I'm sorry I've been a bum. I'll still help you like I used to, but I will move out of here as soon as I can."

She smiles and holds his head in between her palms. "I love you so much, Butchee. I'm just losing my mind in this tiny apartment. Both of us trying to move around in here. Plus, this medicine is making me sicker and messing with my mood. I can't take a damn step without this walker. I just thought you gave up and that pissed me off. You weren't acting like my Butchee. I knew you would figure things out and do the right thing for us. You always do. Just like I was there for you, when your momma died.

Just like I was there for you, when you came home. We have to keep supporting and lifting one another up. I know I have been hard on you, but I just want what's best for you. We're family."

CHAPTER 6

It's getting darker outside and Sherman is still seated against the prison wall. He looks sad with his chin resting on his knees. His shoebox is beside him. He sighs as Officer Vernon and 5 other guards exit the prison.

"You work here now?" Officer Vernon says, sarcastically.

"What? What the fuck you mean?" Sherman snaps.

"Mr. Ford, I was only joking." The officer's smile quickly vanishes as he motions Sherman with his palms.

"I guess those assholes didn't tell you-you could have hitched a ride on that bus." Officer Vernon says as he points to the bus driving off the parking lot across the street.

"You serious? I've been seeing those motherfuckers all damn day." Sherman says with a look of disbelief.

"Look, if you're going to DC, I'll drop you off." Officer Vernon says.

"I'm not riding in no damn backseat." He says, sarcastically. They both laugh as they head to the officers' car, get in and then drive off.

Officer Vernon looks over at Sherman and sees him staring blankly out of the window at the cars on the highway. He turns the radio off. Sherman does not move. "Do you need to call your family? You probably want to make sure someone is home." He says as he pulls his cell phone from his front pocket and hands it to him.

Sherman nods his appreciation before dialing. "This is FBI Agent Page. Who am I talking to?" Agent Page questions. Sherman hangs up the phone and hands it back to Officer Vernon.

"Don't answer that phone if it rings," Sherman says before the phone rings. They both just stared at the phone. Officer Vernon looks at the number. "Why not? This has to be your folks because I don't recognize the number."

"I dialed the wrong number." He replies before staring back out of the window. They drive for another twenty minutes before Officer Vernon double parks in front of a row of houses on a narrow street. Parked cars line both sides of the street in this well- kept, single-family-home community. There are two professionally dressed people standing out on the street.

"I really appreciate the ride." Sherman says as he extends his hand.

"No problem." Officer Vernon replies before shaking Sherman's hand. "I'ma wait to make sure you get in." Officer Vernon says.

Sherman knocks on the door twice. "Wait a minute!" Ella shouts coming down the stairs. She opens the door and stares blankly at him.

He is beaming as he moves in and hugs her. She reluctantly hugs him back. He tries to kiss her. "Hey Baby," he says before she covers his lips with her palm.

"Hi, Sherman." She says as she pulls away and stands in the doorway.

With confusion, he stares into her large eyes that are surrounded by her smooth dark chocolate complexion and attached to her hourglass figure. "Wha-. You ain't happy to see me?"

She folds her arms,"I'm glad you're finally home."

He tries to walk into the house but she presses her fingers on his chest. "I wasn't going to try to kiss you. I was going in the house." He says staring quizzically into her eyes.

"That's why I stopped you," she replies.

"So you're not letting me in the house?" He says with a stunned look.

She shakes her head, "No, Sherman." She sighs, "I allowed you to use my address to help you make parole but you can't live here. I told you this." She says.

He sits his shoebox on the porch and sighs as he wipes his face with his palm before gripping his chin. "So where do I supposed to live?"

She fights back her tears. "I don't know, Sherman. I thought you were supposed to live with E?"

"He didn't even come to pick me up. Are you serious that I can't live here with my woman and our daughter?" He says with irritation.

"Yes. I am. This was your doing? You created this. You're to blame and only you." She says as she whines and wipes tears from her eyes.

"So you don't love me anymore?" He says in a softer tone.

"I do. However that doesn't change our situation."

He shakes his head in disbelief. "Really? So you really don't want anything to do with me?" He says with disappointment.

Officer Vernon pulls into a parking space after a car leaves. He turns on his radio, but occasionally glances at them on the porch.

She smirks and shakes her head in astonishment. "Susan knocked on this door, Sherman. She came to my home where our child resides and tells us you're fucking her. So, she's dead. So it's all about me now?" She snaps.

"It's always been all about you. I don't know why she would tell you some bull-shit like that." Sherman says in frustration.

"Lower your voice on my porch or leave." She says daringly.

He just stares at her. Every emotion in his body is clashing.

"Mommy." says Loretta as she appears in the door. She is the spitting 8-year-old image of her mother. "Daddy!" She says before leaping into his unprepared arms but he catches her.

"Baby, baby, baby!" He shouts playfully as he rocks her and kisses her cheek and neck.

"Stop Daddyyyy. Your making me laugh! Daddyyyyy. Daddy stop." She giggles. He stops. With loving eyes, she says, "Do it again!" He does.

"Stop. Ya making too much noise." Ella says reluctantly.

He kisses her on the nose and puts her down. She wraps herself around his leg. "Are you home now, Dadddddyyyy?" She says with hope and a smile.

Ella looks away. He caresses the back of Loretta's head. "Yup."

"Yayyyyyyyyy! My daddy's home." She sings and does little dances. "Come on, Daddy. I want to show you my room. I put all of my pictures and cards on my wall that you sent me." She says as she pulls his hand.

"Not tonight. You can show Daddy another time." Ella replies.

"Why, Mommy? Why can't I show Daddy now?" She says pleadingly.

"Give him a kiss and go get ready for bed and he'll see you soon." She says.

With tears streaming down her face, "I love you, Daddy. You don't want to live with me?" She says with a heart breaking tone.

His eyes begin to water. He shoots an evil glare at Ella before stooping before Loretta. "I can't at the moment, but we're going to have so much fun now that I am home." He says, forcing excitement in his voice.

"If you don't live in jail anymore and you don't live with mommy and me, where do you live, Daddy?" She says.

He looks up at Ella. "I'll find out tonight."

Ella gently grabs her hand and leads her into the house. She starts yelling and screaming. "I want my daddy! I want my daddy! Mommy! Mommmmmy! Mommyyyy!" She stomps and screams all the way up the stairs and into the bedroom window where she whines for him.

Ella is a nervous wreck. "You did this. You think I ever wanted this for her? It is bad enough she knows what jail is? Now you're home and you can't be with us? You did this?" She says frantically crying.

He reaches to wipe her tears, but she shoves his hands away. "You did this." She says as she desperately tries to compose herself. "I have to go take care of my baby. WE just broke her heart," Ella says as she wipes away her tears, but more tears fall as she steps into the house and closes the door in his face.

He sighs and leans his forehead against the door panel. Then he walks off her property. Officer Vernon blows the horn before stepping out of the car. "Mr. Ford!" He shouts. "I waited to see if you needed a ride somewhere else." He says, sincerely.

"I don't know of any other place to go." Sherman says defeated.

"I know a place."

They drive for twenty minutes before he stops the car in front of a DC Shelter for men. The property looks disgusting. Trash all over the place and a long line of sickly and dirty looking addicts. There are also a few nicely groomed men that have actual jobs standing in the line. The majority of the men are black and of all ages. Sherman glances at the line and looks at him in despair.

"Just show them your papers. They'll make room for you. I know this isn't how you envisioned your first day home, but stay focused. You'll find your way out of this," Officer Vernon says before reaching into his pocket and handing

Sherman $40. Sherman just stares blankly at the money and slowly shakes his head. "Mr. Ford, take it. This will re-assure me that you really want to do right. This money will help you get around or buy some food. I can't stress enough that things will get better if you exercise patience. Don't throw your freedom away because it didn't start off like you envisioned. Take the money."

Sherman sighs. He grabs the door latch as he looks at the lock. "Thank you." He says before taking the money. Then he exits the car.

CHAPTER 7

Butch and Tonya are seated on her living room couch. Her legs curled beneath her body as she stares at him with affection. He is stressed and vulnerable. He avoids her eyes by looking at her forehead, chin, chest and knees. He glances at the clock that reads: 7:30 pm. "I'm done trying. They keep telling me because I got a record they can't hire me. Then my damn aunt is all on my damn back stressing me. 'Give me some money. Give me some money.' I hated being in prison but it's like that's where folks want me. But, I ain't going back. But I'm tired. I'm tired of living like a bum. Motherfuckers forced my hand. I just need to snatch me a quick $200,000 and disappear. That's what I'mma do. Yea.

That's what I'mma do." He is talking more to himself than to her.

She kisses him on the lips. "It's going to be alright, Baby. What's best for you, for us... I'ma hold you down. I got your back."

He leans back and looks into her eyes. "Huh?"

She smiles and kisses him. "I want to be with you, Butch. I think we can have something really special."

"Huh?" He replies with a look of bewilderment.

"Yea." She takes his hands and drapes them over her shoulders. "No more pressure. No more stress. You can take your time.

Whatever you choose to do, I'm here. I want you right here with me." She gestures to the floor.

"Huh? What does that mean?" He says quizzically.

She sits up straight and stares seriously at him. "How do you feel about me?" She inquires.

"Huh? I mean, you cool. Except you took a long time to give me some." He says jokingly in an attempt to change the subject.

"Do you think I'm good enough to be your woman? Cause I think you're good enough to be my man." She replies.

He glances around over his shoulder. "Yea. You cool. I like you."

"I never gave you any drama." She replies.

"Yea, but we've only known each other for two weeks." He replies humorously.

"I'm serious. I'm not telling you that I love you, but I know I easily can. We have a connection. I want to explore that if you're willing? I mean, I really want to have your back as your girl and not as your friend."

"You serious?" He smiles with a look of caution.

"I'm very serious. I want you to move in with me. Don't worry about what you can and can't provide. I'ma hold us down while you find your place in this world."

"I've found my place. It's in these streets." He replies.

"You could do better, but don't bring it home with you. This is our sanctuary."

"Soooooo, I get to hit that as much as I want?" He smiles as he scans her body.

She raises her arms in the air. "If we're official, it's yours. You can do what you want with it."

"Damn." He pulls a condom out of his pocket. "I'm in!"

She grabs the condom hand. "Once was enough with that. This is yours.

He smiles and releases the condom. She tosses it before leaning in to kiss him.

CHAPTER 8

8pm. Inmate receiving area inside of the United States Maximum Security

Federal Penitentiary in Utah. The back wall is three bullpens full of prisoners separated by concrete, plexiglass, and by race. 20 whites, 20 blacks and 15 Latinos. It looks like a zoo exhibit. There are men being processed by guards across from the bullpen.

Charlie is flashing the white power sign at the white prisoners as he mops the floor. A few of them respond with the sign. Charlie acknowledges Skip with a head nod. About twenty of the prisoners in the bullpens are standing around in their boxer shorts or tighty-whitey underwear.

Charlie exits the area as the Warden along with thirteen other administrators enter the area. The Warden stops and looks puzzled at the half-naked men in the bullpen. "Sergeant, why haven't the clothes of these inmates been returned to them after their strip searches?" The Warden questions.

"Sir, those inmates haven't been processed yet." The Sergeant replies.

The Warden looks baffled at the inmates. "Then why are they naked?"

"I am assuming they're waiting to be processed, Sir." The Sergeant replies.

"Raise your hand if you are from Lorton." The Warden says.

Blue Eyes, Rakeys, Big Moe, Black Smoke, Marc, Dre, Skip, Devil, Psycho and the rest of the half-naked men raise their hands.

CHAPTER 9

Sherman keeps glancing back over his shoulder at the dingy, addicted, employed, but broken black men standing, some impatiently, in the shelter line. A young man standing behind plexiglass slides a clipboard with a document attached through a slot in the Plexiglas. Then he hands Sherman a pen. Behind him are shelves full of bedrolls, blankets and dingy looking sheets, and a wall clock that read 8:15pm.

"Sign right there," he says as he grabs a bedroll and drops it in the slot that he opens to Sherman. "Listen up everybody! This is the last time I am repeating this tonight! Check out time is 7 am. You don't leave nothing behind. When you go... everything goes with you. We start allowing folks back into the facility at 7pm. This is a first-come- first-serve facility. We only have 100 beds back there and as you can see, either in front of you or behind you, we fill up pretty fast. I advise you to be in line at 6pm every day to have a chance of getting in. Some of you are lucky tonight and others are not. We already have 76 people back there so some of you won't get in tonight. I'm sorry but you have to get here earlier than you have." He says as men start complaining behind Sherman. "I advise you to get to know others in line, because they'll let you know where they sleep when they can't get a bed." He says before lowering his voice and speaking to Sherman. "Go through those double doors and stake your claim on an empty bunk. Don't leave your valuables lying around, we're not responsible if they are lost or stolen. Fights, stealing and making loud noises will get you kicked out."

He says before handing Sherman a blanket and sheet and points to the double doors.

Sherman walks into the chaos. There are four rows of bunk-beds from wall to wall with narrow walkways. The walls are dirty.

The noise level is alarming. There are men huddled together in between bunks talking, scheming, and laughing. Wet men with towels wrapped around them that are walking from unseen showers. Some men with mental illnesses are wondering around. Cigarette smoke is thick in the air.

Sherman is immediately filled with anger. He sighs and makes his way to a bed in the back and throws his belongings on top of it. Love Boat steps into Sherman's space. His left fingers continually tap his neck. Sherman glares at him.

"You got any cigarettes? You got any cigarettes?" Love Boat says as he rocks and continually open and close his palm toward Sherman.

"I don't smoke." Sherman politely replies.

"Then I betta not catch you with a cigarette, Motherfucker." Love Boat says as he briskly walks away.

Sherman sighs and starts making his bed. A man wrapped in a towel swiftly walks into the aisle. Sherman angrily spins toward him. Consumed with fear, the man's towel drops and he slips and falls. Sherman grabs him by the back of his neck. The man starts slipping and pleadingly as he tries to crawl away but Sherman's grip is firm.

"Please! Please! Don't hurt me! You can have whatever you want! Just don't hurt me!"

Sherman looks down at the bottom bunk and sees that the bed is made. "Is that your bunk!"

The man shakes his head in terror. "Yes. Yes, Sir. Pleeeeease, Man."

Sherman releases him. "My fault. You just ran up on me."

The man swiftly grabs his towel and covers himself as other men start gathering around. Sherman turns back to his bed. The man goes and removes all his stuff from his bed.

"Why you moving your stuff?" Sherman says annoyed.

"I'ma find me somewhere else to sleep, Sir. I didn't mean any harm."

"I apologize. I made a fucking mistake." Sherman replies.

"I just want to sleep somewhere else." The man says before disappearing through the crowd. Sherman stares at the men gathered.

"What? Get the fuck away from me!" Sherman barks.

The men walk away mumbling profanities. Sherman makes his bed and climbs on his bunk. He keeps all of his clothes on. He ties his shoes tighter before laying back on the bed and staring up at the ceiling.

Leroy walks into the aisle. He is an older man dressed in a white uniform and a red hat with a gold chicken on it. The chicken's wings were in motion. Beneath the chicken are the words Fry A Bird. The logo is on the front of the baseball style cap and on the pocket of the polo styled shirt. He has his bedroll in his hand and a carryout bag from his job. "Young Blood, is anybody sleeping on the bottom?" he says.

Sherman looks over at him. "Naw. You good." Sherman replies.

Leroy starts making his bed. "Man, there was some crazy dude just threw his bedroll at the front window and ran out the building in a damn towel. His clothes in his hands. That ass is going to get cold real fast." He says with a chuckle. After he finished making his bed, he stood up. "Young Blood, would you like some chicken?"

Sherman looks at him. "Naw. I'm good."

"You were down Occuquon? You Sherman, right?"

Sherman immediately sits up. Leroy throws his palms in the air. "No beef, Young Blood. I was just shocked to see you here."

Sherman lies back down. Leroy sits on his bunk. "This is a helluva place to end up in. The first time I walked in here it felt like I was transferred from one prison to another. We should never be released to this."

"How long you been here?" Sherman inquires.

"This my third year."

"Three years! It looks like you have a job." Sherman replies.

"I do. I work at Fry A Bird. I've been working there for two and half years."

"So why don't you have your own place?" Sherman says.

"Young Blood, I don't have any credit and I make minimum wage. I can't afford my own place. At least not in DC. Shit, DC is home. I ain't going nowhere else to struggle. I'm trying to figure some shit out. For now, it's all about being patient and remembering this is better than being locked up, even though it's like being locked up. You know what I mean? But it's going to come together. It's going to come together." Leroy says more to reassure himself. "You sure you don't want any of this chicken? I didn't do anything to it. I just always bring enough to share with my new bunk buddies. The shit pretty good. I'm just tired of eating it."

"I'm good."

"By the way, I'm Leroy, Chicken man.

CHAPTER 10

Butch and ten other older killers, drug dealers and professional crapshooters are in a huddle in the empty basement of a crap house. All of the men except Butch have a carrying bag. Butch and Howard are crouched around a pot of money on the floor. Howard cheerfully scoops up the pile of money and stuffs it in his bag. The pair of dice on the floor show two set of 2s.

"Who said Little Joe only comes around on the Fourth of July!" Howard shouts as he collects his money from a few of the other men. Butch is frustrated.

"Who fading me now!" Howard shouts.

"I'm fading you." Butch says annoyed as he drops $3,000 on the floor.

Howard looks down at the money. "The pot is $5,000, Young man.

Butch sighs then drops the rest of his money on top of the pile. "Bet." Butch replies.

Howard smiles at the others before counting and dropping $5,000 on top of Butch's money. Then he squats, scooping up the dice and shakes them before releasing them. The dice spin beside the money before stopping. One dice reads five and the other dice three. "That's my number, Baby!" Howard shouts with excitement. "Bet me $2,000. Who in?" One of the other men drops

$2,000 at his foot. Howard digs back into his carrying bag and counts off $2,000. He drops it on top of the man's money.

"I want in on that bet." Butch says.

"Then put your money where your mouth is, Young Man." Howard replies.

"It's in the car." Butch says.

Howard stares skeptically at him before scanning the room and seeing mixed looks. "I don't want no shit, Young Man. You have it in the car? If not, let's keep it respectable." Howard says.

"I got it." Butch replies. Howard shakes the dice and releases them. One dice stops on the number four. The other one spins for what feels like an eternity be-

fore stopping on the number four.
Howard leaps into the air!

"Got dammit! Got dammit! I told ya this
is my number!" Howard shouts with
glee. He scoops up his money and faces
Butch. Butch is devastated. "You don't
have my money do you?" Howard says
with sympathy.

"I'll get it to you." Butch says with an-
guish.

"I knew it" Howard says before snatch-
ing a gun from his lower back and shov-
ing it between Butch's eyes. "So now I
have to kill yo young dumb ass! Don't
you know better than to play with a
man's fucking money?" Howard says
scanning the room. "Damn. This is supposed to have been a peaceful day for
me. I didn't want to have to kill a motherfucker! This is why I don't like ya let-

ting these young motherfuckers in here. They want something for nothing. "Close your eyes." He says calmly to Butch.

"Don't kill him in here." Old Face shouts walking toward him with the aid of his cane. He has on a polo style shirt with the collar up.

"I'm not closing my eyes." Butch replies. Howard smacks him with the palm of his free hand before swiftly grabbing him by his collar to keep him from staggering. He presses the barrel against his teeth.

"What in the fuck you mean, you're not going to close your eyes!" He smacks Butch again and regards him. Pressing the gun against Butch's left eye.

Old Face eases up beside Howard. "Let him live. Do that for me. Find another way for him to get your money."

"Fuck dat! He done beat me out of two grand. I done smacked him twice and he talking about he ain't closing his motherfucking eyes like I'm playing." He locks eyes with Butch. "Motherfucker, Bye."

Butch immediately drops to one knee. "Please. Please. Please. I don't want to die. I promise you... I'll pay you back. I promise you. Please don't kill me. Please."

"You Bitch ass nigga! You the same bitch nigga with all this I ain't closing my eyes shit. Now you dick level. Give me a reason not to kill yo faggy ass." Howard demands almost showboating.

"Mr. Howard, I have some work on the street. As soon as I get paid, I'll give you your money." Butch pleads.

"How you know my motherfucken name!" Howard barks.

"You're a legend around here. You been getting money forever. I promise you I got you. Imma give you your money in two days tops." Butch pleads.

He smacks Butch again. Butch falls onto the floor. He aims the gun at him. "You're right I am a motherfucken legend. Look at me!" He shouts. Butch looks at him. He whips out his phone and takes a picture of Butch. "Have my money in two days or die in two days. Something is telling me to kill yo ass right now! Get the fuck out of here." He shouts before kicking Butch in the side. Butch exits. "I should've killed that little motherfucker." Howard shakes his head with regret. He puts his gun back and puts his phone in his pocket.

Old Face steps up to him again and pats him on the shoulder. "You did the right thing. You taught him a real good lesson."

Howard shakes his head in regret. "Fuck it. Let's gamble."

CHAPTER 11

The clock on the wall reads 9:35pm when Blue Eyes, Rakeys, Marc, The Devil and three other white men walk into the A side of the housing unit carrying their bedrolls. This is the same unit that Decker killed Bobby. All of the prisoners that are out of their cells are staring at the newcomers.

With his bulging eyes, Brace watches them from his wheelchair in front of the sport's TV. He's deathly thin with dry, dark and peeling skin with sores on his visible skin. His mouth keeps opening. He rolls his wheelchair over toward the black men going down the three steps as the white men walk up to the second floor. He waves his hand toward the black men. "Excuse me, Men.

Are any of you from Lorton?" He says in a weak raspy voice.

Blue Eyes stops and faces him as Rakeys walks up behind Blue Eyes. "Yea. We are. Why? Wussup?" Rakeys says, proudly. Marc stops beside them.

Brace forces a smile. "Wussup, homies. I just want to give ya the low-down about this joint. It'll take about five minutes. Just come back after you drop your stuff in the room. We lock in about 15 minutes."

"We can do that now, Cuzzo." Blue Eyes says.

"Aight. Imma come down the ramp on the other side. What cell you in?" He points to Blue Eyes.

"15, Cuzzo." Blue Eyes replies.

Brace holds up his thumb and rolls his wheelchair down the ramp on the other side of the common area as Blue Eyes and Rakeys walk into their shared cell. They are making up their bed by the time he arrives. Rakeys leans against the desk across from their bunks. Blue Eyes leans against the sink.

"Is it alright if I come halfway in so these crackers and chumps won't be in our business?" Brace says. His mouth stays open after he finishes talking.

Rakeys waves him in. He rolls his chair halfway into their cell.

"Look, there are only a few of us on this whole compound. I mean blacks in general. It's sixty of us. Plus whomever came with ya. Now, it's about three hundred and twenty Aryan Brothers. They run shit and have no problem killing us. Most of the guards are their sympathizers. I'm saying this so you know what you working with. Every time you hear the word Nigga doesn't mean you go to war. These crackers try to provoke us often. Of course, you handle disrespect when it comes directly to you or another homie. Only a few soldiers on this compound and the rest are scared niggas. So, we have to stick together. This ain't no different than Lorton except the rabbit has the gun now. Outside of that, we stick together. Any beefs you have with homies in Lorton, we squash them here. We need every   soldier we can get. It's vicious. These crackers like setting a motherfucker on fire, so keep your cell doors closed at all times. If you take a shower, make sure one of us has eyes on you. They just killed one of their own last night. The damn leader comes strolling in here 4 in the morning. He goes to the cell and kills one of his own. When they find the man in the cell, his cell-buddy was eating him with a bag of Party Mix and a can soda. They shipped that crazy sucker to the looney bin. So be on guard. If they will eat their own, imagine what they will do to us." Brace warns.

"Why ain't this joint locked down, Cuzzo?" Blue Eyes questions.

"Man dead in his cell with his cell buddy eating him, murder solved. Plus, it was two of a kind. If one was black, we would be on lockdown."

"Another thing, the administration considers us the DC Blacks. The crackers consider us DC Blacks. What that means, if they beef with one of us, they beefing with all of us. You have to be on your toes at all times."

"We only have problems with the ABs. Everybody else don't like us but they don't fuck with us. We eat together. We rec together. We walk together. I'm not saying you have to be married to a mother-fucker. You just have to know where your ass is at- at all times."

"The homies are going to get together with the other black dudes and give ya canteen and shower shoes and shit. We all one family. Last thing, everybody does business even with our enemies. The white boys getting the migos to bring in the coke. The Asians bringing in the blow. We bringing nothing, but we got knives. We barely getting visits out here. So, I'mma let ya get settled in and we'll rap in the morning. Ya need anything?" Brace says.

"Yea. Two knives a piece." Rakeys says, seriously.

Brace starts smiling. "I love you already, man."

"Thanks for reaching out. What's your name again, Cuzzo?" Blue Eyes says as he extends his hand.

"My name is Brace. These motherfuckers call me Deadman strolling because I got that AIDS shit. So, I understand if you don't want to shake my hand."

Rakeys eyes widen. Blue Eyes smiles and leaves his hand extended. "I'm Blue Eyes. It is a pleasure to meet you, Cuzzo."

They shake hands. Brace looks at Rakeys, smiling with his hand extended. "You are?"

"I'm Rakeys. We not handshaking." Rakeys says as he walks to his bunk.

Blue Eyes looks shocked. Brace smiles, "We good...Well, Ima let ya be. I'm in cell 30. I have some noodles, steak, fish, and some chips if ya hungry.

"I'm good." Rakeys says dryly.

"I'll take a bag of chips, Cuzzo." Blue Eyes says. Rakeys looks at him in bewilderment. Brace smiles at Rakeys.

"Follow me to my cell." Brace says to Blue Eyes.

CHAPTER 12

Howard, Old Face and the rest of the men from the crap game stroll out of the basement door on the side of the house. Old Face stops, uses his cane to hold himself up and slaps his knees as he looks over at Howard, laughing. He points to Howard and laughs even harder. Howard playfully pushes him. Immediately, Butch appears behind them from the back the house. Old Face's smile freezes as he notices him briskly moving toward them.

"Howard," Butch barks before Howard sees him. Butch fires a round through his forehead. The gushing blood welcomes the second bullet. The other men scramble to get back into the house. Old Face slips and falls onto his back before the third bullet hits Howard in the chest and sends his dead body crashing to the ground. He lands beside Old Face. Butch steps up and Old Face raises his arms to block bullets but Butch fires three more shots into Howard's throat. "Talk that slick shit now." Butch whispers. Calm down, Old man. You good." Butch says as he rummage through Howard's pockets and bag but only recovers car keys and a cellphone.

One of the men returns firing a semi- automatic. Butch fires back as he runs toward the front of the house. The man gives chase but gets tired before he even makes it past the house. At the end of the block, Butch climbs into a red two door sports car. He drives off.

CHAPTER 13

The cell doors bang as they open. Within seconds men all around the unit begin exiting their cells. The Aryan Brothers on the top tier congregate and start a conversation. Then they stare across the tier at Marc as he exits his cell. He's startled but regains his composer and swiftly exits the unit.

Rakeys and Blue Eyes exit their cell. They become the focus of Aryan Brothers. Rakeys steps forward and loosens his muscles before making his chest jump as he stares at them. Devil exits his cell and looks intently at the Aryans. Then he tosses up the Nazi salute by extending his right arm into the air with a straightened hand and shouting, "Hail Hitler." The majority of the others return the salute and repeat the chant. The rest of them flash the White Power sign.

Blue Eyes looks at Rakeys with amusement as Brace races toward them. "Men, don't feed into that. It's just an intimidation tactic." He warns in hopes of changing Rakeys' focus. Doesn't work.

Rakeys continues to glare from floor to floor. "Hard to scare a gladiator." He says.

"It's best to prepare for war before you begin one." Brace says with caution.

"We stay strapped." Rakeys says as he rotates his shoulders.

"Ya got knives?" Brace asked with a look of bewilderment at Blue Eyes.

Blue Eyes has his back against the wall with his hands in his groin area. "Never leave home without them." Blue Eyes responds.

Brace starts grinning. "Ya youn-gens are wild. I love it. But let's chill out." Brace says as he tugs at Rakeys' arm. Rakeys looks at his arm then at Brace.

"Bra, I don't mean no harm but I ain't comfortable with you touching me. You got that shit, right?"

Anger fills Braces eyes but van-ishes just as quickly as it appears. Rakeys notices it. Jon Jon starts walking toward them from the back of the tier. Blue Eyes steps up off the wall and faces him. Brace immediately looks over his shoulder and sees Jon Jon. "Homie! What's up, Jon Jon. These are some other homies from Lorton." He says quickly.

Blue Eyes instantly relaxes. He smiles back at Jon Jon and shakes his hand. Rakeys looks at him and nods his head.

"Too much excitement and the doors just opened." Brace says.

Jon Jon looks around to assess the danger. "Wussup? We got action?"

"No-no-no. Everything good." Brace says.

"You sure? These crackers can get it if they want it." He says locking with some of the Aryans.

Rakeys smiles and extends his hand. "My man."

Jon Jon shakes his hand.

Brace starts laughing. "Shit. I'm hungry. Can we go get some breakfast before we catch a few bodies?"

"Sure. But they going to stop this sucker shit... trying to intimidate men. I'm tired of this shit." Jon Jon says with a raised voice.

"Stay humble. It ain't about them right now." Brace says.

"What's up with this homie shit? When DC dudes start saying that bamma ass shit?" Rakeys barks with irritation.

"It's a bad habit I picked up from being around all these out of towners." Brace says.

"Well, you need to cease that bamma shit." Rakeys says.

They lock eyes. "First of all, you ain't going to keep saying slick shit to me. I got AIDS but ain't no bitchassness in me. I can dig it if you uncomfortable with my disease but what you ain't gonna do is disrespect me any mother-fucking more."

Brace says as he eases to the tip of his chair.

Rakeys glares at him. Blue Eyes grips their shoulders. "We in a room full of enemies and ya about to attack each other." He says.

"You right. My apologies. This black on black crime shit has got to stop." Rakeys says humorously. They all start laughing. Brace turns his wheelchair in the opposite direction. "I'll catch ya by the exit. I have to go to the ramp."

"I'll push you. We'll meet ya by the door." Jon Jon says.

"Naw, Cuzzo, we roll with ya just in case the white boys want to work out." Blue Eyes says.

The compound is full of men exiting six housing units and heading to the kitchen or waiting on others. They are grouped together by race. Correctional officers are positioned throughout the compound. There is a higher concentration of them near the route of the prisoner's journey to the kitchen.

The gym is at the top of the compound with the kitchen to the right. The library is next to that, then the school, and then shops are next to it. The administration building takes up the bottom half of the compound. In the center is a huge field that is the size of a high school football field. The top corner is covered with black asphalt and has a basketball court with two rims. The bottom end of the field has the shape and accessories of a small baseball diamond. The middle area is grass where they play flag football or just hang out. At the top of the field, in between the building, is the gym.

Big Moe runs up and hugs Jon Jon when he recognizes him. "Awwwwww. How you been man!"

"Trying to keep my head above water. You still singing?" Jon Jon says laughing.

"You know it!! Awwww. It is so good to see you." Big Moe says.

"Where John and Sherman?" Jon Jon says still smiling. Brace and the others stare with a look of surprise that matches Big Moe's. "Man, John is dead and Sherman is on the streets." He says visibly uncomfortable as he shakes his head.

"Dead? John? I'm surprised Sherman is home then. I can't imagine him not catching a life sentence for killing the dude who got to John."

"Sherman's not suicidal." Rakeys says.

Jon Jon looks puzzled. "Huh?

Moe genuinely squeezes Jon Jon's shoulders. "It's a long story but Sherm had to kill John."

"Huh?" Jon Jon is completely baffled.

"Keep it moving," one of the guards barks.

"Huh?" Jon Jon struggling to understand.

"Sad shit." Big Moe says visibly disturb.

"Damn. Two good dudes. Damn." Jon Jon says with disappointment.

"I'm Brace." He says to Big Moe. Big Moe extends his hand.

"Pleasure." Big Moe says.

Brace pauses. "I got AIDS, Big Moe. You may not want to shake my hand."

"Fuck that. I can't catch that shit from shaking your hand." Big Moe says laughing hysterically as he shakes his hand. The rest of them introduce themselves to each other as they walk into the kitchen. The prisoners have a rule that they sit with people from their own state, gang, or race. All the black men are seated together.

CHAPTER 14

Sherman's clothes are wrinkled and his eyes are bloodshot red. He walks down the sidewalk as Ella and Loretta exit their property holding hands. Loretta snatches free and dashes toward her father. Her bulky book bag bouncing on her back. She leaps into his arms. He lifts her and plants kisses all over her face. She giggles and tries to dodge his kisses. Ella frowns as she heads toward them. "Come on, Loretta! Sherman, we have to go. I have to get her to school on time so I can get to work....on time." She says with forced irritation.

He puts her down. Ella grabs her hand and shakes her head disapprovingly of his appearance. "Let me walk her to school." He pleads.

"No." Loretta's smile vanishes and she stares sadly at the ground.

"Why?" he replies.

"1: you don't know where the school is, and 2: you look like you had a long night. Focus on you. She is good. I got her. She will always be ok."

"I only want to spend some time with her by walking her to school."

"Mommy, my school is only around the corner." Loretta whines.

"No..." She sighs. "You can ride with us. Then I can drop you off somewhere close-by because I have to get to work." Ella says with reluctance.

Loretta excitedly jumps up and down. They walk to the car. Ella gestures for him to get into the backseat with Loretta. He sighs. They get into her car and she drives slowly. Sherman focuses on Loretta.

"What is 2 + 2?" He asks.

"4, Daddy!" She shouts gleefully. "Daddy, that's too easy." They laugh.

"Ok. What's 5x5?"

"25!" She immediately shouts.

"You are soooo smart. Okay. One more. What is 1,600 divided by 234?"

"I'ma have to get back to you with that one, Daddy." Loretta says as her parents immediately start laughing.

He reaches over and hugs her. "You are too funny." Sherman says, still laughing.

Ella parks in front of the school. The area is full of cars, parents, students and staff.

"We're here." Ella says looking at Loretta.

"Mommy, can Daddy walk me to the door?" Loretta pleads.

"Oh, now you're not a big girl. You don't usually want Mommy to walk you to school but now you want Daddy to walk you. Wussup with that?" Ella says jokingly.

"Mommmmmmmmy, everybody knows you. Nobody knows I have a Daddy."

He lowers and shakes his head in shame before kissing her on the forehead. "I am so sorry that nobody knows you have a Daddy. I am so sorry."

"It's okay, Daddy. I forgive you. Mommy said that God forgives you. Mommy will forgive you sooner or later. Sometimes I make her mad but she always forgives me. You just have to be good, Daddy, and she will forgive you too."

Both of her parents are near tears. "Little Girl, it is time for you to get into that building." Ella says with a quiver.

Loretta grabs his hand and leads him out of the car. She immediately starts introducing him to her friends and staff. He lifts her up into his arm and kisses her on the cheek before she walks through the metal detector. Ella blows the horn at him as he walks pass the car.

He walks over and she rolls down the window. "Where are you going?" She asks.

"I have to go see my parole officer on K. Street." He replies with his hands in his pockets.

"Get in." She says. He grabs the back door. She blows the horn and gestures for him to get into the front seat. He gets in and they drive off. "You were out partying all night?" She asks.

"Naw." He says, looking straight ahead.

"So, what's your plan?" She questions. "To get back with my family."

She shakes her head with a look of disbelief. "You wouldn't have to get back with your family if you kept your dick in your pants."

He shakes his head. "I'm not trying to argue with you."

"There is no argument. You created this situation. Ain't no coming back. I've moved on."

He locks eyes on her. "Pull the fuck over." He says as he grabs the latch.

"No...How you feel right now is how I felt when Susan left my house. The same house where all your belongings are. That same house where your daughter and I waited for you while you didn't wait for us. That same house where that little girl cried almost every night. Finally, got her to stop and you do that to us. Now she's crying again because you're free and you can't come home because you chose another woman over us." Ella fumes.

"You fucking another dude around my daughter?" He barks.

"That's all you heard?" She says with a look of disappointment. "What do you think? Don't ask questions you really don't want the answer to." She replies.

He looks out the passenger window. "Let me out."

"I will as soon as we get to K street. I keep my word." She says, sarcastically as they continue to drive through the DC streets in silence.

CHAPTER 15

Psycho, The Devil, Skip and Barbwire are leaning against the outer gym wall flanked by 19 other Aryan Brothers. Barbwire is humongous with a bodybuilder's body, bald-head, and five visible barbwire tattoos on his body. One of the tattoos is on each knuckle, two are around his arm muscles and one wrapped around his neck. The neck tattoo has AB in the center of his throat. Then there is Charlie, stooped in front of the new men.

Activities are taking place all over the compound. Mostly men of color are playing basketball. Cartel leaders, mafia leaders, Asian leaders, black kingpins, and other gamblers are all smoking cigars as they play card games near the housing unit.

The rest of the prisoners on the compound are walking around, working out, or huddled together. There are guards positioned around the compound and in the tower monitoring all movement. Blue Eyes and the other new blacks are gathered near the basketball court with the black shot-callers. They are receiving bags of canteen.

Weirdo and other Aryan Brother's start to join Charlie on the wall. Weirdo is a slim guy in his thirties with solid muscles and bulging eyes. One of his eyes is blue and the other is brown. He has a crooked smile with hundreds of tattoos all over his body except for his neck.

Charlie is looking up at the four new white guys from his stooped position as he toys with a small branch. He notices Psycho's focus is on Blue Eyes' group. "It's pretty simple. I'm fair but I run a tight ship. I don't interfere with how you make your money. Just know that the Brotherhood is your support system and you must support the Brotherhood. We take care of our own around these parts and we crush any resisters. Niggas, spicks, yellow-backs, disloyal ABs, the guards, or even the president of these United States, if he mess with the movement. Any questions so-far, Brother's?" Charlie says.

"So, you're in charge of the Brother's?" Devil questioned.

Charlie chuckles, "No, Sir. The Brothers don't need that. I'm more of an overseer. Does that answer your question, Devil? I tell ya...that sure is a mighty frightening name."

"Yes, yes you did, Brother."

"Brothers, we need to maintain our stronghold and visibility in this institution. Without it we lose our advantage. It would serve the Brotherhood well if you, Skip, would take a position in the kitchen. Devil, if you would take a position in lockup as a janitor and Psycho if you would take a position in the library as a clerk." Charlie says as he watches Psycho still staring at the group of blacks. "I'll take care of that before the week's out. Brother, Psycho, your focus is bothering me. Are ya ok?" Charlie questions with a forced smile.

"Finally, it is good to outnumber these niggas" Psycho replies.

Charlie squints at him before scanning behind him at Blue Eye's group. "Awww. They're alright. Those some good house niggers. Occasionally, we have to make'em eat they dicks but we really don't have too many issues with them. Now...I heard ya came down here with some Niggas that ain't been housebroken. Field Niggas. We'll straighten them out as time goes on if they act out. Now do ya have any issues with these Niggas?"

"Yea, we're at war. Skip slaughtered and dragged one of theirs proudly in front of them. We couldn't finish them off because we all got put on lockdown. Their true leader got released but that half breed over there named Blue Eyes took his place. He's a problem." He says nodding toward him.

Charlies looks over there. "Well, they don't appear to be at war. But, we'll get you some knives by the end of the day. Now ain't no war until either I sanction it or it's forced upon ya. For now, we'll just look at the Niggas on some gangster shit." He chuckles as he spins around to face where Blue Eyes and the others are huddled together and just stare.

CHAPTER 16

Sherman slouched in the chair in the waiting room with seven other black men from ages 19 to 63. The 63 year old is talking to the 19 year old as another guy is entering the building and being directed by a security guard to walk through the metal detector.

"You have to figure out how to make your P.O. a part of your plan. It's the only way you're going to keep your freedom," the 63 year old man warns.

"What you mean make'm a part of my plan?" The teenager replies.

"They the only people that have to be in your life until your parole ends. Your momma, your girl, your kids, and everybody else can stop fucking with you, but your P.O. ain't going nowhere. They may give you a new one but you'll always have one. So accept that and piss when they say piss. Come see them when they say come."

"Man, but I'm free -" the teenager was saying.

"Naw. Parole means you're just doing your sentence on the streets. You still serving time. Just add what they want to your life. It'll make your life easier."

Ms. Fox appears inside the doorway. "If Mr. Ford is here, please come with me."

Sherman glances at the clock and it reads 2pm as he stands and follows her. After she sits behind her desk, she gestures for him to sit. "Ummmm. Can you put me in a halfway house?" He says with hopelessness in his voice.

"No, Mr. Ford. You were denied halfway house because of your violent history."

"That should have been more reason for me to go. Now I'm homeless. I live in a damn shelter." He says, barely maintaining his frustration.

"We verified your home address. If you had told the truth, we wouldn't have released you into homelessness. But ya be so in a rush to get your freedom. I can actually violate you, but I'ma cut you a break. My suggestion is that you call around to your family and convince them to let you move in or get a job, stay in the shelter while you save your money and get you an apartment."

"Can you help me get a job?" He pleads.

"Mr. Ford, I'm not trying to be a hard ass. You have to prove yourself before I use my resources. I can't help you and you make it bad for me to help people who are doing right. So far, you're not looking too good. You're home for twenty-four hours and you're really already in violation. For now, I will allow you to live in the shelter but you have to get a job."

"Allow me? I don't have nowhere else to go. And I don't live there, if I don't get there in time to get a bed, I guess I have to sleep in the streets."

"Then I suggest you get in that line on time to get you a bed. It's all about following the rules. I'll see you in three days. I have to meet with other clients.

CHAPTER 17

Butch strolls into his Aunt's house. She is stepping into the kitchen with her walker. She stops and affectionately looks at him. "There's my Butchee. I haven't seen you in two days."

He looks withdrawn as he lowers his head and kisses her on her cheek. She holds his head with her hands, steadies her weight by holding him. "Look at me, Butchee. What's wrong?"

"I don't want to hustle or rob. I tried to do the right thing, Auntie, but it's not working. What should I do?" He says.

"Butchee, you have a special skill-set. You don't qualify for a job that can pay you what you're worth. You're not like me. You're not the book smart type. School wasn't for you." She says with compassion.

"But, Auntie, I was doing good in school. I was getting A's and B's." He replies re-assuringly.

"You're not dumb. When I got hurt, your real skills came out. You hit that street and instantly you found your place. That money had been waiting for you. So, don't you question why you don't fit in. You're above a regular job. You're not like me. Butchee, I was so proud of you the other day when you rolled over and gave me $15,000! $15,000! No job can give you that in one night! Nobody else in this whole community knows how to do that, but you do! You know where the money is. That's what you're good at. Don't fight to be someone else. You were miserable looking for a job, but when you decided to do what you're good at, you hit the lottery. Don't fight who you are."

"So, you're saying be a criminal?" He said with confusion.

"You're a hustler. Do what you do best. Now what's really going on with you?"

"I need to borrow a $1,000."

"A $1,000...for what? Where's all that money you made?" She says with anger as she goes and opens a cabinet.

"I was gambling. I was trying to double if not triple my money."

She frowns and shakes her head. "I can't help you, Butchee. I used that money to pay off bills. Your bills: phone calls from prison, clothes, rent and money to put down for my new house. I need more money, Butchee; you'll figure it out. I know you will. I believe in you." She says as she starts preparing to make breakfast.

CHAPTER 18

Black Smoke walks away from Marc and Dre seated on one of the benches on the compound. He starts rubbing his hands as he approaches Charlie and Barbwire walking on the track.

"Champ, can I rap with you for a second? Ya know what I'm saying?" Black Smoke says as he licks his lips and rubs his hands.

With baffled looks, they stop and Charlie points at himself. "Are you talking to me?"

"Yea. Yea. I want to holler at you for a minute. You know what I'm saying." He says as he licks his lips again and rubs his hands.

Before he walks over to him with a smirk, Charlie gestures for Barbwire to stay. This grabs the attention of all the men on the compound. Their body language indicates they expect trouble. Black Smoke extends his hand but Charlie ignores it. "What's on your mind, brotha? Charlie says, sarcastically.

"That wasn't called for. Ya know what I'm saying. I come in peace." Black Smoke look at him forcing a smile as he rubs his hand and licks his lips.

"I don't know. I don't understand that language." Charlie says annoyed.

"I hear you're the Man on this compound. Ya know what I'm saying," he says as he licks his lips and rubs his hands. "I am trying to see how we can work together to make it beneficial to us both."

Charlie giggles. "How do you see us working together?" Black Smoke takes a step forward and Charlie leans back and gestures for him to go away. "Look, Brotha, you new here and you don't know how things operate. You can't be walking up on me. I'mma nervous redneck." Charlie says smiling.

Black Smoke notices his buddies stand. He signals them to stay. "Yea. I get it. I'm black and you're white. We suppose to hate each other but that doesn't have nothing to do with making green together. Ya know what I'm saying." He licks his lips and rubs his hands. I heard you making moves. I got all of the black behind me. They move when I say move.

There will be buses on buses of us pouring in. Ya know what I'm saying." He says licking his lips and rubbing his hands. We either mix well or we don't. I can hold down the black on my end but I need my palms greased. Ya know what I am saying?" Black Smoke says licking his lips and rubbing his hands.

"I'll keep that in mind as well." Charlie says as he rejoins Barbwire. He playfully rubs his hands together and licks his lips as he glances over at Black Smoke.

CHAPTER 19

Butch is driving up Martin Luther King, Jr. Ave., SE and spots Sherman walking out of the Social Security Building with several pieces of papers in his hand. "Hey, Sherman! Sherman!" He screams in pure excitement as he slams on breaks. "I'm so glad to see you out here."

"How you been?" Sherman says.

"I'm good. You need a ride?" Butch rambles.

"Yeah. I'm not driving."

"Cool jump in so we can rap." Butch says with excitement. Sherman climbs into the car and Butch pulls over to the curb. "So how long you been out here?"

"Five days." Sherman says as he watches two voluptuous curvy women walk pass the car wearing super tight jeans.

"Damn. Five days. I know your wife and daughter are happy as shit."

Sherman just nods his head in agreement. "How you doing? You working?"

A solemn look covers Butch's face. "Naw. I tried. They won't hire me."

"Why, your record?" Sherman inquires.

"That and I don't have no fucking skills. Plus, you need a damn G.E.D, high school diploma or a college degree or something out this bitch. I can't even get a fucking minimum wage job. All I got is a record. Lorton ain't prepare us for this bullshit." Butch replies.

"You must be eating. This joint have paper tags." Sherman replies.

"I'm taking chances. If I catch a bamma slipping, I'm punishing him." Butch says with no regrets.

"Damn. I thought you would be the one to make it out here." Sherman replies before an alarming look takes over his face. "What time is it?"

Butch looks at his watch. "It's 6:30."

"Can you drop me off on 4th street by the court house?"

"Sure." Butch raises his seat and drives off. They continue to talk until Sherman gestures for him to pull over in front of the shelter. Butch looked quizzically at him. "What you getting from here?"

"This home for the moment." Sherman says reluctantly.

"What the fuck. What's up with your peoples?" Butch says.

"It's a long story." Sherman.

"Damn." He rubs his eyes in frustration. "Shit. I don't have a damn dime or I would put you in a hotel. Shit. I just lost all of my money in a crap game last-night. Damn, Sherm."

"It's cool. I hate this place but I'm working on two locations to go to. For now, I have to endure this shit." Sherman says, dryly.

Butch shakes his head. He looks as though he is near tears. "Man, I don't even have a spot to take you. My living situation is fucked up. Shit. You want to sleep in the car? I'll stay in this joint with you."

Sherman starts smiling. "I appreciate that but I'm going on in this joint. I have to get in line so I can get in." Sherman says as he grabs for the door.

"Hold up, Sherman. I'ma call this chic now and ask her can you crash with us. I can't leave you like this."

"Do this...talk to her tonight if she says yes, I'll stay over there tomorrow."

Butch whips out his phone and saves Sherman's number. Then Sherman exits the car. Butch stares in despair, as thunder shoots across the sky. Butch drives off as Sherman looks up at the sky.

CHAPTER 20

Psycho is being loud and boisterous on the top tier in front of a group of Aryan Brothers that includes Barbwire and Weirdo. They stare with amusement and in awe as he talks in his clinging tank top that reveals hundreds of colorful tattoos on top of his huge muscles. Some of the men below, trying to watch TV, are annoyed, but no one is saying a word.

"I told him, go ahead to the Feds. He grabbed her by her neck with his gigantic hands and squeezed the piss, shit and farts out of that Nigger lover. She was dangling like she was hanging from a tree. It reminded me of the good old days. He demonstrates the squeezing.

"Where were the other guards?" Barb-wire says with anticipation.

"They were counting on another tier. It didn't matter because they knew...I die for my men. They probably wanted her dead. She fucking and sucking all these Moooon- keys. Anyway, he had her pinned to the bars and squeezed so hard that his knuckles had bar prints and pieces of her flesh was attached to his palms. One of the whore's eyeballs popped out. He dropped her like a piece of shit when it was all over and came back to the cell. The monkeys couldn't believe their eyes. I told those scared niggers, "We don't have no rope but we got plenty of white palms for any nigger that has something to say. She laid there for about another hour. I'm surprised none of those niggers ain't pop their cells to have sex with her. They be so damn excited to get their disgusting hands on a white woman. Now if one did, I would have laid him beside her."

Big Moe and Dre are leaning against the wall across from them but on the bottom tier. They're watching all of the movement.

"When the guards see all the scratches on him, they shipped him to the Feds. I don't know what facility he's in, but he is a helluva soldier and Brother... that is all you should be proud of. He would die for the cause. This is the kind of loyalty I expect and the kind of loyalty I give. Me and my boys made tons of money down Lorton. How many of ya are getting a fair share around here?" He looks at Barbwire and he lowers his eyes along with some of the others. "Shit! If you're happy with it, I love it! We're the Brotherhood, all for one..." Psycho shouts as the others join in.

"One for all!!!" The Aryan Brother's shout.

One of the cells they are standing in front of opens and a Spanish guy sticks his head out of the door. "Yo, Bro, bring down the fucking noise. I'm trying to fucking sleep." The man says as he stares threateningly into their eyes. Then he closes his door behind him.

Psycho loosens his neck. Barbwire stops him and nods to the other men. They quickly retrieve two sheets, two other men grab the ends and they block the view of everyone else in the unit. Then Barbwire taps Psycho on the shoulder. He snatches the Spanish guy's cell door open. Before he could step into the man's cell, three other Aryans move quickly pass him. The Spanish guy was lying on the bottom bunk. He tried to jump to his feet but they pounced on him. They were beating and kicking him senseless. Psycho pushes his way pass them and whisks the man off his feet by his neck. He strangles him against the wall until his body dangles lifeless.

"C.O. C.O. C.O. coming." Weirdo whispers.

They quickly lie the corps in the bed and covers everything except his head and exit the cell. Two Aryan's that were in the cell start wrestling while the sheet is up. The guard comes and snatches one of the sheets and sees the two men wrestling.

"What's this shit! Ya break it up! Break it up or I'm calling the code." The guard shouts.

The two men release each other and start laughing. "C.O., we were only wrestling. We were trying to see who can get the other on the ground first."

"We don't tolerate horse-playing. I'll give you two options: 1. Both of you lock in for the night, or 2. Ya going to the Hole," he demands.

The two men walk to their cells.

CHAPTER 21

Sherman is walking down the street in the heavy rain with his head down, his shoulders up and his hands in his pockets. He glances at the sign on the shelter's door, "No Empty Beds". He shakes his head and walks to the corner and stops at the traffic light near the 3rd street tunnel. Above the tunnel is the Department of Labor. Cars are whisking by in both directions.

Love Boat instantly appears beside him holding a large piece of roofing tarp above his upper-body. He stares at Sherman with wild eyes. Sherman eases his right hand out of his pocket and makes a fist. "Great Beast, a lion needs a den from the elements of death." Love Boat barks.

"What? What the fuck you say?" Sherman says frowning.

"Give me a cigarette." He says with an open palm as his finger seems to move uncontrollably. The tarp falls onto his head and covers his face. His palm remains open.

"Man, stop asking me that dumb shit!" Sherman says with rising anger.

Love Boat repositions the tarp as he faces a man walking up in their direction from behind. Sherman spins toward Love Boat, almost throwing a punch until he sees the approaching man. "Give me a cigarette!" Love Boat barks at the man. The man briskly crosses the street. Love Boat turns back to Sherman. "A lion needs a den from the elements of death." He says firmly at Sherman before tossing the tarp off of his head. Sherman leaps back in a fighting stance. Love Boat just points to the tunnel as he stares into Sherman eyes. Then he walks off into the street without looking at the traffic and nearly gets hit. He disappears into the tunnel.

Sherman stares bewildered until a car speeds pass and water from the street splashes all over him. He stumps his foot and curses at the car before taking a seat on the stoop on the side of the building. Tears start streaming down his face. He drops his hands onto his knees and just stares at the ground in total humiliation and defeat. He looks up when he detects movement from his peripheral vision. It's Love Boat standing at the edge of the tunnel but not in the rain. He is staring directly at him with those wild eyes like a parent waiting for an unwilling child. Then Love Boat motions like the Incredible Hulk and screams but Sherman is unable to hear what he is saying. Then he disappears back into the tunnel.

Three cars speed by and water leaps on to the curb. Sherman gets up and runs over to the tunnel. He stands at the entrance. It is well lit with cars driving into the tunnel beside him. A car moving recklessly through the tunnel honks its horn and Sherman presses his body against the wall. He stares down the tunnel. He does not see any sign of anyone. Then he notices a balled up empty packet of cigarettes fly out from what looks like a slit in the wall. He sees a crawl space. He peers into the darkness.

"Great Beast, there is no one here but cubs." Love Boat's voice echoes from inside the wall.

Sherman makes fists and eases into the opening. He cannot see anything but he is stepping on all kinds of trash, bricks, buckets, old mattresses, and a body that leaps up. Then a female voice curses at him. He leaps back in total fear. A match is lit and almost instantly a fire inside of a large bowl illuminates a limited space. He spots Love Boat's face as he leans in and lights a cigarette between his lips. He leans back exhales clouds of smoke as the tip of the cigarette sizzles. His wild eyes seems to soften as he reveals decaying top teeth and no bottom front teeth. He raises his arms in victory and laughs out loud.

Homeless people started moving around, sitting up and walking toward him. "Let me hit that. Let me hit that!" They beg.

Love Boat leaps into some kind of battle stance as he puffs his cigarette. "Beware the Beast is present. You move you will be devoured by his lust for fresh meat. Let me be or I will be forced to slay all you worthless motherfuckers." He laughs.

The homeless woman Sherman stepped on shouts from the darkness. "Fuck you, Crazy Motherfucker. If you don't give me a puff of that damn cigarette I'ma whip your crazy ass."

"Come Beast, your crown awaits you." He says motioning Sherman towards him. The woman steps at Love Boat's side, taking a drag of his cigarette before

Love Boat directs Sherman's attention to some cardboard laid on the ground beside him. As Sherman, slowly sits, Love Boat starts staring up talking to invisible people. No sounds are coming from his mouth, but smoke is coming from the woman's mouth as others congregate around her. She starts passing the cigarette around. Then Love Boat storms off as if he is leaving with the voices in his head. Sherman leans his back against the wall and watch the seven homeless people gathered and taking turns puffing the cigarette. When the cigarette and the fire dies out the people stumble back into the darkness. For the first time being home, he feels some form of content, but his eyes, remain alert in the darkness.

CHAPTER 22

Charlie stops in front of cell ten and the electric door creaks as it starts to open. He sees Psycho standing erect with his shirt off and facing the door. He looks prepared for war. Charlie smiles at him and leans on the door frame after the door is completely opened. "Hey, Brother, how are you holding up this morning?" Charlie says without emotions.

Psycho sighs and goes and sits on his bunk. "I don't know how they pulled me in for that shit."

"Stand when you're addressing me." Charlie barks.

Psycho looks at him with a hint of irritation before sighing and pushing himself up and facing Charlie. Charlie glances down the hall before releasing the mop and walking into the cell. He stands a few feet away from him. The cell door rocks as a sign of the guards not wanting him in there. "Psycho, I don't appreciate you s-i-g- hing like you don't want to stand for me. Is there something you and I need to take care of right fucking now?" Charlie says with intensity.

"I don't have a problem with you, Brother." Psycho says with a sinister grin.

"Ok, because this would be the best time to deal with it." Charlie says as he scans Psycho's eyes. Then he steps back into the doorway, smiles up the hall and waves at the hidden guards. "Brother, I know you ran things where you came from. I get that. We all have to learn to make adjustments to be able to survive in these unpredictable environments. I can't tolerate you or anyone else making moves without my approval. I just spent the last fucking two hours with a Mexican leader trying to persuade them that their guy was in violation, forced our hand, and that it doesn't benefit them to seek revenge because we would unfortunately have to kill everybody. I don't like those fucking conversations all just because you were talking smack outside of a fucking cell! We're established here. Everybody knows we run shit! You don't have to fucking prove yourself! I have already accomplished that for us all. Then the Mexican and I had to reassure the Warden that we're not at war. Fucking told him, it was a beef against two men and not four! This is not without penalties to US. One of the Brothers you

excited is on a flight to ADX [1]so you and
the rest of the brothers can go back onto
the compound. A senseless sacrifice of
one of our men when the prison is changing complexions, and we're fucking in
debt with Mexicans for $4,000 because
you wanted to flex. This is my final
warning, Brother, without my word, it is
a death sentence. See you on the compound."

---

[1] 1 ADX is a supermax prison in Florence,
Colorado. It houses the most dangerous
inmates.

CHAPTER 23

The cell door opens and shuts three times mechanically. Rakeys looks up from sipping his coffee on his bunk. "School time, Son." Rakeys says, jokingly.

"Fuck dem, Cuzzo. How they going try to make me go to school, Cuzzo!" Blue Eyes snaps from underneath the covers.

"The same way they forced your young ass here." Rakeys says, jokingly. "C'mon, Son. Brush your teeth, wash your face and where is your homework?"

Blue Eyes yanks the cover off of his head. "Stop with that son shit, Cuzzo." Blue Eyes barks.

Rakeys burst into laughter. "What's with going to school?"

Blue Eyes wipes the wax out of his eyes as he sits up. "Because I have 40 years to life in prison. What the fuck I'ma do with a G.E.D.? They just need to leave me the fuck alone, Cuzzo. I'm try-ing to chill, but between them and these fucking white boys with this nigga shit, I'ma go off."

The doors repeat. Blue Eyes leaps off the bed, puts on his shoes and ties them tight. He snatches a 7 inch shank from under the toilet. "Fuck them! They can get it now!" Blue Eyes says as he struts toward the door. Rakey's grabs him by his arm. "Hold up, Killa. Let me holler at you before you declare war over this shit." Rakeys says, jokingly.

"Fuck this joking shit, Cuzzo!" He says in a rage.

Rakeys' smile vanishes. "C'mon, Blue, don't give up. I put your appeal in. You got a good shot of giving some of this time back, if not all of it. I understand your frustration. Shit, I have four life sentences... and two of those I caught down Lorton for killing two motherfuckers when I was frustrated just like you are now. Don't throw in the towel. You still got a shot. It's a fucking G.E.D. class. It's not the death penalty. Plus, getting this shit, could help you."

"How, Cuzzo?" Blue Eyes barks.

"Shit. It may not help with the appeal but it may help with the Reconsideration Motion. The judge will see you trying to do right, may convince him to lessen your time. Plus, programming can help you get into a lesser security. Lesser security means more privileges. Plus, the G.E.D. isn't a bad thing."

Blue Eyes sighs as he puts the knife back. "I ain't good in school, Cuzzo. That's why I dropped out. I couldn't get that shit. I'm dumb as shit, Cuzzo. They put my ass in special ed. Then bammas started making fun of me. So I started setting they asses on fire."

"You started setting them on fire?"

"Yea, literally, Cuzzo. I wasn't trying to kill them but I was setting their hair, shoes, coats and anything I had time to light a match too." Blue Eyes says without cracking a smile.

"Blue, your young ass been crazy! You can't be setting people kids on fire and shit, but you ain't dumb. You using words like 'literally'."

"Sheeed, Cuzzo, I heard that shit from you. Me saying it is one thing. Just don't ask me to spell it, Cuzzo. These Crackers told me I was reading on a 3rd grade level when I took the test here. I ain't going back for that shit. They going to be asking me what color is the fucking fire truck, Cuzzo. Fuck dat." Blue Eyes says, half-jokingly.

"So, you dropped out in the 3rd grade, Blue?" Rakeys asks in disbelief.

"Naw, Cuzzo. I dropped out in the 9th. I told you they put me in special ED. I rarely went to school and they still passed me, Cuzzo. I don't remember turning in one piece of paper. That school shit never made sense. They wouldn't even help me, Cuzzo. They giving me work with pictures and shit on it. I ain't coming there for that shit. That made me feel stupid as fuck, Cuzzo."

"Damn. I got you. Don't even trip." Rakeys' says reassuringly.

A guard steps in the door as it slides open. "Mr. Albert Marshall?"

"That's me." Blue Eyes says.

"School." The guard says as he jesters with his thumb down the hall.

"I ain't with that." Blue Eyes says firmly as Rakeys looks at him with a look that says, what?

"Mr. Marshall, you have that option or you can go to the hole until you turn 21. As long as you're under 21 by federal law you have to participate in school." The guard says as he grabs his handcuffs off his belt. "Which way are we going... the hole or school?

Rakeys taps Blue Eyes on his shoulder. "Go to school. Just bring your homework back." Rakeys says with reassurance.

Blue Eyes stares threateningly into the guard's eyes before looking at Rakeys and sighing. "Aight. I'm going to school." He says in disappointment.

Rakeys smiles, "Good. Your clothes are in the gray drawer. This is gray." He says as he laughs and taps on Blue Eyes clothes locker.

"Fuck you, Cuzzo!" Blue Eyes says laughing.

CHAPTER 24

"Mommy, who is that dirty man sitting on the steps." Loretta says with a level of discomfort as she steps out of the house on to the porch. Ella quickly steps out as Sherman turns around. A look of brokenness covers his face.

"Hey, Baby, it's daddy." Sherman says with embarrassment.

Loretta sprints down to him. "Don't hug me. I don't want you to get your clothes dirty before school." He says before kissing her on her forehead.

"Daddy, I don't care you're dirty. You're my daddy. I want a hug." She pouts as Ella approaches.

"Daddy is right, you don't want to get dirty before school." Ella says.

"Mommy, I want to hug my daddy. Dis my daddy." She says in defiance.

Sherman smiles and stoops before her. She wraps her arms around his neck and kisses him on his nose. She bursts into laughter and jumps backwards as he tickles her. "Daddy, you playyyyyyyy too much!"

"How are you doing, Ella?" He says as he smiles at her.

She scans his appearance. "Rough night?"

"Daddy, you work in construction now?" Loretta asks honestly.

"Daddy isn't working yet." He replies.

"Why are your clothes so dirty then?" She questions.

"Stop asking your father all these questions." Loretta says.

"Can I walk her to school?"
"No, you can ride with us." Ella replies.

They drive to the school. Loretta grabs his hand. "Come on Daddy, walk me to the door."

"No, I need to talk to your father. There goes Kelly. Go catch up with her." Ella says to Loretta in a no nonsense tone. Loretta hugs her and him and races through the crowd of kids to catch up with her friend.

"Are you ashamed of me?" Sherman questions.

"I don't want anyone questioning her about your appearance. This is her school. These are her friends. This school knows way more than they need to know about her life. I don't mean any harm but you look terrible." She says with compassion.

He lowers his head and sighs. "Don't you think I know this?"

She looks startled, scans the crowd and drives off. "So, you're ready to make a scene at her school?"

He stares out of the window trying to control his patience. "You can drop me off at the corner and I'll walk. I don't want to embarrass you any further." He says coldly.

"No." She says without looking back at him. He glares at her. "What?"

"You need a shower and a change of clothes. Then you can go where ever you have to go." She says firmly. She takes him to her house where he showers and exits the bathroom with only a towel on. He stops at the entrance of her room. She is ironing a shirt. A pair of male pants and a packet of boxers are laid out on the bed.

She looks over her shoulder at him. "Those are your pants and under-wear. I'm ironing your shirt. Your tennis shoes are over here by my feet. You're going to have to correct the shoe strings. You can leave those clothes you had on in the bathroom. I will throw them away unless you want them. If you do, I'll wash them."

He smiles. "Thank you." He goes and holds the pants up to examine them.

"They fit. They're yours." She says as she picks up the shoes and shirt and walks over to him. He drops the towel and pulls her to him. He immediately becomes erect. She grabs his erection and smiles. "Somebody is happy to see me."

"I'm always happy to see you. I miss you so much. I love you more than I love anything except our daughter. I want you right now." He says lustfully as he caresses her body through her clothes. He kisses her. She kisses him back before dropping the things she was carrying. She leans her head back and he begins to kiss her neck. As he begins to unbutton her shirt, she holds his wrist and stares lustfully into his eyes. "You ready to tell me the truth?" She says before kissing him.

"You know I love you. You're not doubting that?" He mumbles.

She stares into his eyes and presses her lower body against his erection before kissing his chest. She starts stroking his erection as she lowers herself to her knees. She licks the base of his penis as he is consumed with emotions. "I'm so horny. Baby, I know you love me and I love you. I miss you too but I am talking about Susan. Are you ready to tell me the truth about her?"

"I've told you the truth." He says as he caresses the side of her head. His head is tilted back and his eyes are closed.

She releases him and stands. She walks over to the door and stares back at him in the same position she left him. He opens his eyes after a few seconds and looks down in confusion. He stares over at her in the doorway. "What?"

"Can you put your clothes on? I have to go to work." She says sternly.

"Huh? What? What's going on? I thought we were about to..." he says pointing at his erection.

"We were, but you changed that. Come on. Get dressed." She says.

He walks over to her and caresses her shoulders. "You don't want me? I want you so bad right now." He moans in her ear.

"You don't want me bad enough. You keep lying to me. Get dressed. We both have to go." She says with irritation. His penis deflates and he goes and gets dressed.

CHAPTER 25

Butch is seated on the front porch of his building. He is staring sadly at the ground when a shadow blocks out the sun. He looks up.

"My Man. How you doinggggg, Buddy?" Mailman Mitch says.

"Mailman Mitch." Butch says smiling.

"Go head, Man." Mailman Mitch says laughing. He has on his mailman uniform, a stack of mail in his hand and a mail bag draped over his shoulder. He is a short middle aged man with muscular shoulders, bald head, goatee, a little pouch stomach. He has a silver pinky ring on each pinky and a hoop silver earring in his left ear. "How you doinggggg, Man?"

Butch stands and shakes his hand. "I'm making it."

"Hey. Hey, ain't we all. Let me tell you something, it's going to get better. You watch. You just keep doing what you're doing." Mailman Mitch says as he stares seriously, but reassuringly into Butch's eyes.

"Can I ask you a quick question?"

Mitch puts his right foot on the step and his elbow on his knee. He gives Butch his full attention. "Surrrrrrrrrrrre. Wussup?"

"Why the fuck you so happy?" Butch replies.

Mitch burst into laughter. "Looka here, Mannnnnn. Long story short, I got a good one. When you got a good woman. You hear me. I mean a gooooood woman, you can't do nothing but smile and be happy and shit." Mailman Mitch says with glee.

Butch nods his head at his building. "This motherfucker here always trying to make me take vitamins and shit."

"Shit. That's what they do. They make us take better care of ourselves. I say you got you a good one. If you know like I know, you better keep her. Take the pill. Shit. It ain't like she trying to make you do no dumb shit. She looking out for you. Answer this...would you be taking the pill without her giving it to you?" Mailman Mitch questions.

Butch just shakes his head no.

Then Mitch rubs his belly. "Look what mine did to me. I was skinny ass hell before my Baby. She taking too good of care of me. She got me too healthy. Hell, I'ma keep eating as long as my Baby is happy. We good. Got me a youngster too. Fineeeeeeee. Big bone too. Country big bone. You hear me? Man, sounds like you got you a good one. They hard to find out here." Mail-man Mitch says before reaching into his mailbag and pulling out a sheet of paper. "Oh, almost forgot. Hear ya go." He hands the paper to Butch.

"You kept your word. Thanks for the job application." Butch replies.

"Ya know. If I give my word, hell, I'ma keep it. Fill that out today and give it to me tomorrow. I'll put a word in for you too." Mailman Mitch replies.

"I just came home about a year ago."
"From the joint?"

"Yea. I was down Lorton." Butch says in a softer tone.

"Ya know. Man, that's behind you now. That's your past. Shit. We all did some-thing. I did my little dirt when I was a youngsta. Got in trouble too. When I got this job, I stayed out of them streets. Then I got my Baby and I been hitting good every sense. So...leave that back there in your past."

"I had a body. A body on a cop too. You think the Post Office will hire me?"

Mitch rubs his forehead. "That's a tough one, but looka here, we won't know if we don't try. They may say yes or it may go the other way. Now, if you don't try, you telling yourself no. Look, I think you're a good youngsta with a good head on your shoulders. I'ma put a word in for you. It may help. You may not need the help. We gone try." Then Mailman Mitch pulls out his card and hands it to him. "Mannn, if you not busy at 5:30 tonight, I want you to go to this meeting with me. I think it would be right up your alley. I really do. I think you will like it. Ya know."

Butch smiles as the door open. Tonya steps halfway out of the door. "Bae." She says as Butch turns around and opens his mouth. She smiles and

presses the pill on his tongue before clos-
ing his mouth and kissing him on the lip.
He looks at Mailman Mitch. Mailman
Mitch smiles. "You got you a good one.
Let's get this mail to these people. Ya
look gooood together too. Go head,
Man." Mailman Mitch says as he stands
to get pass them.

"Tell him again." Tonya says, playfully.

Mailman Mitch starts giggling.
"She fine too.

CHAPTER 26

The apartment door opens.

"Yes. How may I help you?" Zoya says with a strong Ugandan accent.

"I'm here to see my mother." He says, dismissively as he tries to walk by her but she gently presses her palm against his chest.

"Who is ya Modda?" She says, politely but firm.

"Mrs. Ford." He replies as he stops trying to push by her.

"Whud is ya name?" She demands.

"Sherman Ford." He utters.

She burst into laughter as she places her palm over her chest. "Awwwwww. You da good boy who did bad tings. Ya modda talks about you all dee time. I am Zoya. Her home health-care aide. I take care...good care of ya modda. Why are you out? You is sup-posed to be in dee prison." She laughs.

"I got released. Can I see my mother now?"

"Yes. But I must warn you. She is very sick. Her heart is very, very bad. She cannot take any stress. She already stressed about her good bad boy. Any problems ya have...you need to keep dem to yo'self. She only needs happy stories. Ok?" She says with a smile.

"Yes." He says reassuringly.

"Follow me." She guides him to his mother's bedroom and motions him to stand out of sight. His mother is watching soap operas from her hospital bed. "Mrs. Ford, I have a good surprise for ya. It is a very good one. Are ya ready for thee surprise?

His mother looks at her with exhaustion. "Yes. What is it?"

"It is a man but not that kind of man." Zoya says, playfully.

"That kind of man would kill me." Mrs. Ford says jokingly.

"Come. Come." Zoya ushers Sherman in.

A huge smile takes over Mrs. Ford's face. She uses her remote control to raise to a sitting position.

"Momma." He says with a child's innocence as he rushes over to her waiting arms. She hugs him as tight as her strength would allow and kisses him on his cheek.

She starts patting the bed for him to sit. He sits. "How are you, Baby?"

"I'm good. How are you, Ma?"

"God is so good. I'm getting stronger every day. I prayed and prayed for you. Now here you are. Where you been?"

"Huh?" He says with confusion.

"You been home a few days. E called me. You were supposed to stay with him. So, where have you been?" She says with concern.

"You talked to E?"

"Yes, Zoya has the number for his wife. Give it to him, Zoya. E is in F.B.I. custody. Where have you been? You don't look like yourself. You look stressed and dirty." She says.

Zoya coughs. He looks back at her.

"Zoya, hush. Don't listen to her. I'll worry more if you don't tell me."

He drops his head in disappointment. She caresses his hands.

"I've been staying in a shelter."

"A shelter? No. No. No. You're not going back there. You live here."

"Mrs. Ford, you cannot do dat. This is a section 8 apartment. They have rules. When I helped you extend your lease, it stated that no one- with felony convictions can live in the residence. You been to prison, ye?" She says looking at Sherman. He lowers his eyes. "You cannot stay. No, good son, would want to have his elderly and sick modda evicted. No? " Zoya warns.

"To hell with them. I pay my bills on time every month. This is my apartment and this is my son. He grew up in this house! I said, he is living with me and that's final." Mrs. Ford barks.

"Ma, don't get upset. I'm trying to get back in the house with my family. I can't live with you." He replies.

"Well, until she lets you back in there, you're staying with me."

"Mrs. Ford, why don't you speak to the rental office manager and get permission. Do this the right way so you do not cause problems. Your health is very, very important and it is very, very bad. Talk to them."

"Well, get them on the phone." Mrs. Ford barks.

Zoya calls the rental office and hands the phone to Mrs. Ford. She takes the call and has a brief conversation before hanging up.

"He'll be in tomorrow. He is a good man.

"For now, your Sherman can stay at the shelter until the manager says it is ok for him to stay here." Zoya warns.

"I'm fine, Ma. Don't worry." Sherman says.

His mother pats his hands and looks sadly at him. "I'll work this out tomorrow. This is your home."

"No stress, Mrs. Ford. We will call tomorrow." Zoya comfortingly says.

"Ma, don't. I'm good. If they say that I can stay tomorrow, I will. For now, I am good."

"Zoya, can you fix my baby something to eat?"

"Yes, Ma'am." Zoya says before exiting the room.

CHAPTER 27

Butch is seated in a school auditorium next to five older men and fifteen boys between the ages of 11 - 16. Mailman Mitch is standing in front of the boys. "It's been a long night but a good-night. We do this because we love you young brothers. We just want you to make something of your lives. Ya are smart, young and handsome young men. Ya know. It's sad to see other young brothers throw their lives away. Ain't nothing in those streets but trouble," he says before a thirteen year old raises his hand. Mailman Mitch points to him. "The floor is yours, Simon."

"What if trouble comes to us? What are we supposed to do?" Simon questions.

"What do you think you should do?" Mailman Mitch responds.

"Get'em before they get me." Simon responds matter-of-factly.

"What could happen if you do that?"

"I can't get killed if I get them first and I ain't afraid of prison."

"With that kind of thinking, that's where you will end up. Remember we talked about the school to prison pipeline?" He looks at Simon.

"Yea. That's when we spend more time in the principal's office for punishment than we do learning in the classroom. So eventually, the school calls the cops and we get locked up for fighting or we drop out and start committing crimes. Didn't you say, that they know how many prison beds they will need based on our 3rd grade test scores?"

"That's correct. My point is, with the comment you made before this brilliant one, you already decided prison is where you're going." Mailman Mitch replies.

"No, that's not what I meant. I meant, why should I wait for them to creep up on me instead of getting them first, because I know they're coming for me. I rather go to prison than be carried by 6."

"Shawty! I'm sorry." Butch says.

"No. No. They need to hear from you. Come on. Come on up or say what you got to say from your seat." Mailman Mitch says.

Butch sighs. "Shawty, Simon? Look I just got out of prison. When I was on my way down Lorton it was a bus full of us 17, 18, 19 and 20 years old. As soon as the bus pulled into the prison, they rushing a dude out that was stabbed a whole lot of times. He had a knife in his eyeball. They said he died in the ambulance. Then my buddy Yesterday was stabbed to death by a white racist who isn't even a racist. They made him one in order for him to survive. He killed my friend and dragged his body pass all of the black's cells, screaming, White Power! Simon, people was dying almost every week in there. My cell buddy hung himself because he was so miserable. I mean, you can't sleep because you're expecting somebody to come and kill you. You can't trust nobody. Friends killing friends. You think you're their friend from the streets, but prison changes people. You think you can handle it, but you may be surprised that you really can't. One of my best friends was raped and I couldn't even help him. You don't want that life, but if you looking for it, it's waiting for you. That's all," Butch says with a look of despair.

"Thank you, Brother. That was real. They needed to hear that. We all needed to hear that. I'm sorry you had to live that and carry that madness around with you." Mailman Mitch says with compassion. Then he looks at the boys, "Ya have a choice. Just think about everything we talked about, but really remember what Brother Butch just lived. He's just a little older than you all are. Mr. President, you want to close us out?" Mailman Mitch says.

The president stands and Mailman Mitch sits. "I want to thank all of you for coming out tonight. Like Mitch said, we're here for you. We're here because we really care about you. You might not believe it, but we do. We know all of you are capable of doing great things. You have to want it. It's the only way you're going to get it. Everybody stand and hold hands," the president says and waits for all of them to form a circle and hold hands. "Repeat after me: I am somebody...My first responsibility is to my life. From my good health, my good spirit, my good actions and wise decisions, I can accomplish my purpose. Being the good example I want to see allows me to see a good man at all times. Through my good example I can inspire someone else to be their best selves. My decisions impact my life and the lives of those connected to me. My community's decisions impact our future. We can build a better world together but I must do my part." They chant along with him. Then they clap and start leaving. The president walks over to Butch. Butch is talking to Mailman Mitch who is beaming proudly at him.

"Excuse me, Gentlemen. I just want to shake this Brother's hand," the president says to Butch. "Man, you set this place on fire. Welcome home."

"Thank you, Mr. President." Butch replies.

"Butch, man, Call me Kevin." They both laugh.

Then Simon steps up to Butch. "Excuse me, Mr. Butch." Simon says hesitantly as he offers his hand for Butch to shake.

Butch turns, shakes and holds his hand. "Wussup?"

"Ummm. Yesterday was my favorite cousin." Simon says.

CHAPTER 28

The early morning chill has the men moving swiftly across the compound headed to work and school. Psycho and Devil are walking up the compound.

"My patience is thinning with this twig." Psycho says.

"Don't start a war you know you can't win, Brother. And stop wearing your animosity on your shoulders so everyone can see. You'll force his hand."

"I'm winning his men over." Psycho says.

"Every smile doesn't mean loyalty. It could represent a false alliance."

"I appreciate your loyalty." Psycho replies.

"Don't allow your eagerness to rule destroy your ability to plan properly or see what is happening around you." The Devil says. He spots Blue Eyes walking with a group of black men toward the school.

"What do you mean?" Psycho responds.

"He underestimates these Lorton Niggers. They may not be the smartest but they're deadly. They're like you, they can't accept not being in charge. Sooner or later they'll strike to regain leadership. It would be wise if you lay back and they'll attack for you. They always aim for the head because they think that's where the power is. They believe you and I have fallen from grace so we are not the threat unless you keep having incidents like the one in the library. The best plan you can ever create is the illusion of submission." Devil says.

Charlie comes towards them pushing a large rubber green trash-can with a broom inside it. There are large black plastic bags dangling from his belt. As he approaches, he flashes the White Power sign. They respond as Charlie holds Psycho's hand and stares in his eyes. "How are you, Brother?"

"I am fine, Brother. I am at peace unless you give the word that peace is no longer what's needed." Psycho replies.

"I appreciate that and your leadership. Brother Devil, you rarely speak. Are you adjusting well?" Charlie questions.

"Yes, Brother. My words are secondary to the Brotherhood. I hope it isn't a sign of disrespect?"

"No, not at all. I plan to meet with both of you leaders to get your opinions on what I am missing here and how we can remove those weaknesses. We're a unit and I need to tap into your outside views and strategies. I'm a simple country boy with a lot to learn. You have to be patient with me. You two have operated success-fully in more deadly environments and you can help us make the adjustments we need to make to remain strong."

The Devil nods his approval. Psycho smiles. Charlie taps them on their shoul-ders and rolls the trashcan away.

CHAPTER 29

"Damn. Three months. That's a long time to live in a shelter." Butch says with regret as he drives through a rich community of mini- mansions.

"One day is too long." Sherman replies," If I get this job at the chicken spot, it'll help me get right."

"If you tell your girl that you was fucking that correctional officer, you would have never ended up in the shelter in the first place." Butch says, sarcastically before coughing hysterically.

He laughs. "You got me there. So, you didn't get the Post Office gig?"

"Naw. My record strikes again." Butch said with regret. "That shit stopped me and my girl from getting a bigger apartment too. I can't catch a break."

"Why ya need a bigger place?" Sherman questions.

Butch nods his head toward Simon on the backseat, staring out of the window with his earphones on. "I got a kid."

Sherman back at him, laughing. "Shawty, won't leave your side?"

"Naw. It's cool. His home situation isn't the best and he has too much of Yesterday in him. I'm just trying to keep him out the streets.

"Yea, if he has any of Yesterday in him, he can be a serious problem." Sherman playfully taps Butch on his shoulder. "I'm proud of you for stepping up. Now that's the Butch I know. That dude that was running around with those guns ain't the one I met down Lorton."

Butch swiftly shakes his head no and nods his head toward Simon. "The earphones are on but he listening to everything. Ain't that right, Simon?"

Simon looks at them and pulls the earphones off. "Huh?"

"Nothing." Butch replies. Simon smirks and goes back to what he was doing.

Butch parks in a huge driveway of a seven bedroom house. Sherman whips out his phone and dials a number. "I'm outside." Sherman says on the phone before hanging up. A few seconds later, he exits the car as a woman with long black hair and an amazing figure leaves the house. She has on a satin bathrobe and carrying a gray and orange book bag.

"Damn!" Simon says as he snatches his headphones off and leans his head forward. "She bad. Who is that?"

"Calm down. I don't have a clue." Butch says.

"It is so good to see you." She says as she briefly forces a smile and hugs him. "This is the money for the lawyer. It's actually $21,000. He wanted you to have a $1,000 for yourself. The address is in the bag." She says after handing him the book bag.

"I would bag that and make her tap out." Simon says with excitement.

"He didn't have to do that. How is he holding up?" She folds her arms and looks at him with despair. "He's acting strong but he isn't as strong as you are. They didn't give him a bond. He's already been indicted under the RICO act for running a criminal enterprise."
"Stop with the disrespect. If you're going to be hanging out with me, I don't tolerate anybody being disrespectful. You dig?"

"You acting like she can hear me." Simon says in defiance.

Butch glares at him. "What the fuck I say? I'm dropping you off? "

Simon slumps back in his seat and puts his headphones back on. Butch continues to stare at him. Simon looks down and mumbles, "We clear."

"What you say?" Butch says with a warning tone.

"I said we clear! Damn." Simon says glaring back at him before looking down at his hands.

"Damn. How is the lawyer saying it looks?" Sherman replies.

"He said he put in a Discovery Motion so he really won't know what they have until the judge grants the motion. He was under investigation for 13 years! 13 years."

"Shit. Did he say that they mentioned me?" Sherman asks.

"No. Well, at least not yet." She says.

"What you mean, not yet?" Sherman says with deep concern.

"I mean, no they haven't but they locked up twenty-six people. Some of those people I haven't seen in years. But you should be fine. I just need you to get this money to the lawyer. He's charging us $110,000 to represent him. I already gave him $50,000. E wanted you to take this to the lawyer so you can get a feel of him. Other than that, E wanted you to keep your distance, that's why he didn't want you to stay here. Oh, he said, he apologizes for not being able to pick you up. See, he always thinking about everybody else. He is a good person. Do you think they will convict him for this?"

"I hope not. How are you holding up?" He says with genuine concern.

"I'll be fine. They froze our bank accounts. Luckily he had some money hidden elsewhere because they came here with a warrant and confiscated all the jewelry, all his cars, $30,000 cash, all the pictures of ya from back in the day and all kinds of other stuff. They be following and taking pictures of me like I am a criminal. But I don't care!

I just want my husband back." She says as she begins to cry."

He hugs her again and scans the area. "It'll be alright. Look, let me go and drop this money off. You just hang in there."

She nods her approval. "You're a good friend. Where are you staying because you can come and stay here like you were supposed to. They already searched the place everything should be good now."

"Naw. I'm good." He kisses her on the cheek and gets in the car. "Let's go."

"Everything good?" Butch says as he backs out of the driveway.

Sherman keeps looking around. "You good?" Butch questions again.

"I'm good." Sherman says. "Drop me off at this address." Sherman says after giving him the sheet of paper he just pulled out of the book bag.

As they drive off Butch slows down when he notices Quality in a wheelchair being off loaded in an Ambulance three houses down from E's house. The others do not notice anything. They ride in silence until Butch parks the car in front of a high class building. Sherman digs into the bag and pulls out a wad of money.

"Damn!" Simon blurts out as he moves up to the edge of his seat. "You got that real bag."

"This my man's lawyers office. I have to drop him off this bag. He gave me a grand." Sherman says before counting off $300 and tries to hand it to Butch.

Butch waves the money away. "You need it more than me. Keep it."

Sherman looks at the gas tank. "Man, you don't even have gas. It's the least I can do for you giving the dude at the shelter $50 a week for my bed."

"I'm good." Butch says dismissively.

"I'll take it!" Simon blurts out.

"Sit back!" Butch barks.

"Little Yesterday is wild." Sherman says.

"Not while he is with me." Butch reassures him.

"Good. I won't hold you up. I'll catch the bus to get back to the shelter."

Butch glances at his watch. "I'll wait."
Butch coughs uncontrollably.

CHAPTER 30

Guards are positioned around the back wall. Fifteen graduating prisoners with blue cap and gowns with gold trim are seated in the center of the room. The warden, a captain, and three teachers are standing beside a podium. Refreshments are behind them. Forty happy white family members are seated off to one side and twenty prisoners in their regular inmate clothing are seated on the opposite side of the graduates. Rakeys, Brace, and Jon Jon are amongst them. Blue Eyes looks uncomfortable in the front row.

"Our final graduate to receive his high school diploma is also our valedictorian, and the most improved student with the second highest scores in our educational history.

Ladies and Gentlemen I present to you Mr. Albert Marshall!!

Blue Eyes receives a standing ovation as he proudly accepts his diploma and shakes the hands off all the people standing by the podium. Rakeys runs and embraces him. One of the guards takes a step toward them but the warden waves the guard off. Blue Eyes shakes the hand of a few of the men on his row before taking his seat.

"Graduates, please stand." The Head of Education says. "Ladies and Gentlemen, I would like to present to you this year's high school graduates!!" He points to them and they toss their caps into the air.

Everyone claps in celebration. "At this point we will enjoy refreshments. Graduates, if you do not wish to join in the refreshments, you can return to your housing unit. Congratulations everyone. Enjoy your day. Remember same rules apply as if you were on a visit. Brief hugs and kisses are permitted. We are allowing you to hold your children's hands. Keep it clean. We would hate to end this celebration. Last thing, graduates, no food or drinks are permitted to leave this room. Enjoy." The captain says before gesturing everyone toward the refreshments.

Brace and Jon Jon follow Rakeys as he hugs Blue Eyes. "Man, you did it!"

"Yea. I did. Can you believe it, Cuzzo!" Blue Eyes says with excitement as he shakes all of their hands.

"Not only did you do it, you broke records!" Rakeys says proudly.

A young woman taps Blue Eyes on the shoulder. "I just wanted to congratulate you on your graduation and high scores!" She says staring into his eyes and rubbing his shoulder.

"Umm. Thank you." Blue Eyes says sheepishly.

"Wow. You have some beautiful blue eyes." She says flirtatiously.

"Thank you." He says, shyly.

Weirdo walks over with his cap and gown on and grips her shoulder. "Sara, we over here." He says staring disapprovingly into Blue Eyes' eyes.

"Oh. Ok. Nice to meet you, Mr. Albert Marshall." She says as she rubs his shoulder one more time before walking over to the picnic table.

Rakeys looks at him as the four men exit the room. "Damn. She remembered your name. I didn't even remember that. Nerds get all of the chics."

"I hope I don't have to kill that white boy, Cuzzo," Blue Eyes says, seriously.

CHAPTER 31

Charlie, Skip, Psycho, Devil, Barbwire and four other Aryan Brothers are gathered around one of the benches outside the last housing unit near the gym. They are watching Black Smoke, Dre and Marc happily greeting 19 new arrivals from Lorton Penitentiary walking onto the compound. Brace is rapidly spinning the wheels on his wheelchair to get to them. "Those are the stickup boys of Lorton. Oh shit. Here comes the girlie boys. They are trouble. The fat one is Suga and the skinny one is Nancy, who makes shanks. They're alliances of Blue Eyes. "Both are killers," Skip says.

Charlie looks questionably at Skip. "Of Blue Eyes? Really?

"Yea. They gave him the knife he used to kill the man that raped him and every other shank he had." Skip says matter-of-factly.

"The Nigger Smoke was telling the truth. Huh?" Charlie says, smiling.

"You can't trust him. It's the truth about Blue Eyes, but he's the reason we went to war. I killed a kid name Yesterday because he tricked him into robbing my cell. Now, after the rape, Blue Eyes killed or ordered maybe seven to nine murders. Including six of our Brothers."

"You don't say... Now don't you worry about the Nigger Smoke." Charlie replies.

"How many niggers we have now? I'm very uncomfortable."

"120. This includes these nineteen." Barbwire replies.

Charlie sighs. "Skip, mix their food. Make it a slow kill. Give Blue Eyes something extra. He owes us a debt."

Skip nods his head as Psycho spots Bear and four other Aryan Brothers exiting the Control building with their belongings. Bear looks even bigger than before. Brace is rolling beside Suga.

"Ahhhhhhhh. Bear! Excuse me, Brothers, I see some of my top soldiers." Psycho says before pacing quickly down the compound toward Bear.

"Who?" Charlie says, looking over at Skip.

"Good, Brother. He likes heroin but he's a soldier. They all stand with us."

"Is Bear the one that killed the nigger lover guard?" Barbwire says with groupie excitement.

Skip nods in agreement. Charlie looks at Barbwire with skepticism. Then he sees Bear hugging Psycho, lifting him off his feet.

"I can't wait to meet him." Charlie says with an even tone.

CHAPTER 32

Sherman is gently pushing Loretta in one of the three occupied swings. Her legs are kicking at the evening sky and above the head of kids racing around the playground. Ella along with a half dozen mothers are seated on a wall watching their kids play. Other parents are giving chase to their smaller children or demanding that their kids stop playing dangerously on the equipment.

"Daddy! Daddy, I want to go higher! Push me faster!!" Loretta shouts.

"Ok, one more time. I'm tired." He says with animated exhaustion.

"Time to go. You have to get ready for bed." Ella says.

"Mommyyyyyyyyy. Ok, Daddy, one more time. Go fast!" Loretta shouts.

He runs and holds her way in the air. "Daddy! Daddy! Put me down!!!" She shouts in fear.

He does. They giggle. Then she runs and walks up the concrete on the opposite side of the forty steps and railing leading to the parking lot.

"Be careful!" Ella shouts but Loretta ignores her.

"She's such a tomboy." Sherman says as he laughs.

"So, did you get it?" She says looking at him.

"Yup. I start tomorrow." Sherman replies. "Congrats!" She says with a smile.

He warmly takes her hand and looks at her with deep affection. "I want to come home." He says.

"Really? Do you have something to tell me?" She says with a sarcastic smile.

He sighs. "I got the job." He replies. She shakes her hand free of his.

CHAPTER 33

Tonya is wiping his forehead with a warm cloth. His eyes pop open.

"Good-morning, My Love." She says with unmasked concern.

He feels around underneath himself at the wet bed. "Damn. Did I pee on myself?" He says as he gets up and rips the covers back and sees his side of the bed soaked. He feels his forehead with the back of his hand. "I don't have a fever."

She starts patting his back with the cloth. "It's hot in here."

He kisses her hand that is holding the cloth and takes it from her. "Thank you." He removes his boxer shorts and wraps himself in a towel that was hanging on the closet door. He notices the digital clock next to the TV. "Shit. I have to get him to school. He did spend a night, right."

She hugs him and snuggles her head in between his shoulder and neck. "Yea. He's in the living room." She says as she kisses him on the neck. "I love you." she says with almost a whisper.

He eases her off of him by her waist and gives her a quick peck on the lips. "I know. I love you too." Then he walks into the living room and sees Simon fully dressed and writing. "Wow. You're up?"

Simon smiles, "Yea. The early bird catches the worm. And I had to finish this homework." He says and refocuses back on the homework.

"My man." Butch says before disappearing into the bathroom. She comes up behind him and wraps one hand around his waist and tries to put the pill in his mouth. He moves and shakes his head no.

"You need to take your vitamin." She says with a no nonsense tone and look.

He jogs out of the bathroom and returns in seconds and holds up a bottle of Flintstones Vitamins. "I'ma take these. I grew up on them." He says proudly.

"Yea, when you were three to seven years old. These are grown man vitamins. Open your mouth." She demands. She tosses the pill in his mouth and snatches his vitamins. He flexes his muscles in the mirror. "I'm getting small."

She kisses his back. "That's because all you do is run the streets and don't eat. This is why I make you take vitamins...Oh, one of my friends works for a guy that owns some apartment buildings. She said, 'If we can pay six months in advance, he'll overlook the criminal record." She says.

"How much is that?" Butch replies.

"$1,300 a month. I know you don't have that but it is a way we can get around your record."

He shakes his head. "Damn."

She wraps her arms around his waist from the back and kisses him on his back again. "Don't stress over this. We will be ok. We just know now that it's about who you know in this town. So, we just have to get to know more people so you can get a job." She kisses him once again. "I'm proud of you."

He looks skeptically at her. "Why? What have I done?"

"You've been home almost two years. That's something to be proud of."

He smirks. She kisses him on the lip as his phone starts ringing. He runs and answers the phone. He returns in two minutes, looking frustrated.

"Who was that?" She says with concern.

He turns on the shower. "My aunt needs some money."

"Why she keep asking you! She need to live within her fucking means or get a job! You better not do no dumb shit. Fuck her. I hate her!"

He glares at her. "Don't ever disrespect her. She was there for me when nobody else was!"

"She did what family is supposed to do. Fuck her. She be asking you to take fucked up risks like a no good friend will do. If she wasn't your aunt, you would know she ain't shit." She says with frustration.

He gets in her face almost nose to nose. "Stay in your lane."

"My lane! My lane! I ain't doing nothing but loving and supporting you. You are my damn lane!" She says before storming out of the bathroom and slamming the door behind her. "You need to change

your damn number!! I hate her trifling
ass!"

CHAPTER 34

Charlie is singing and playing a guitar on an elevated stage inside of the gym. There is band equipment behind him. Guards are visible around the compound and throughout the crowd of prisoners in front of the stage. Aryans are standing all in front of the stage dancing or nodding their heads to the music. The blacks are spread out in separate packs. Blue Eyes is leaning on a pillar outside of the kitchen. Rakeys, Big Moe and a few other guys are around them. Big Moe is really enjoying himself dancing.

Black Smoke is deep in conversation with twelve Mexican Mafia near the gym. Marc and Dre are focused on Black Smoke as thirty other DC teenagers are either having side conversations, scanning the crowds, or beatboxing.

Suga, Nancy, and a group of diverse homosexuals are dancing seductively in the center of the crowd. They have their shirts tied to one side, wearing homemade lipstick and other makeup on their faces. Admirers including Barbwire are standing around them either gawking, dancing, or glancing at them from time to time. Brace is trying to engage Suga in conversation but Suga is ignoring him

"I was born on a farm in Mississippi. And where I am from you don't see a lot of strangers. And as kid, I had a wondering mind. Like jumping on my horse and have a race against time. My folks say I was bad as can be but the truth be told all I wanted was to be free... Yea, I'm countreee! I'm a countree man that ain't never been changed! yea, I'm Aryan!"

He sings and the Aryans roar in appreciation. Big Moe pauses with a shocked look on his face. "I'ma country man that ain't never been changed. Yea. I'm countreeeee!" He sings the chorus again as he notices Black Smoke with the Mexicans. Big Moe is dancing happily again and Psycho is with his Lorton Aryans gathered off to the side, away from the stage. "Yea. I'm countree! I'm Aryan Man, that ain't never gone change! Thank you." Charlie says as his set comes to an end and he bows to the audience.

He receives a rockstar applause from The Aryans. Big Moe even claps.

Rakeys looks at Big Moe with suspicion as Charlie leaves the stage.

"Suga, I love your moves. We need to get together soon. I have some moves too." Brace says with a sexual tone.

Suga rolls his eyes. "Dead Man Strolling, please leave me alone. I don't want anything you have."

"Awwww. Don't be like that." Brace says, playfully.

Suga grabs both armrests on the wheelchair and leans threateningly towards Brace's face. "Bitch, you are starting to annoy me. I am not blind. You fucking dying of that shit and you want to kill me. Leave me alone or it will not end well for you."

Brace smiles. "I didn't know eczema was considered a deadly disease."

"This is something new I wrote. I hope ya like this." Jon Jon says into a wireless mic as he walks along the stage. The Aryans greet Charlie cheerfully as he joins his men in front of the stage. He looks at Jon Jon and smiles and nods. "Cut my music on." Jon Jon says. His hard hitting instrumental rap music comes on. He starts prancing around the stage as most of the blacks, especially the youth come closer to the stage. Suga focuses on Jon Jon. Nancy gently smacks Suga on the shoulder as if he likes Jon Jon. Brace just stares lustfully at Suga. "Dudes want to do what they do, be who they see, be all they can be, but ain't nothing in those streets but the penitentiary." Jon Jon raps in full performer mode. The youngsters start happily jumping up and down in the crowd! Even Black Smoke is enjoying it. Blue Eyes takes a step forward to walk to the crowd then he motions Rakeys. "Come on. He doing his thing." Blue Eyes says, cheerfully.

Rakeys rubs his stomach. "My body is fucked up. They serving us spoiled food."

Rakeys says. A few of the other men agree with him. Then he waves Blue Eyes on. Blue Eyes followed by Big Moe and the other men get closer to the crowd in front of the stage.

CHAPTER 35

Sherman is dressed in his Fry A Bird uniform as he sweeps the restaurant dining area. There are three booths on both sides of the walls in front of the service counter. Leroy the Chicken man is ringing up one of three customers in line, and a family of three is eating in one of the booths.

Ms. Fox boldly walks into the restaurant with her badge around her neck and a jacket with the parole emblem embroidered on the back. She stops briefly in front of Sherman with a police officer. "Where is the manager?"

"What's wrong? What I do?" He questions with a look of concern.

"Mr. Ford, I need to speak with the manager and get a urine sample from you. She demands. The police officer looks as if he doesn't want to be there.

"He in the back. Ms. Fox, you see I am working. Why you need to talk to him. I only been working a week."

"You're telling me how to do my job now? Just have a seat. Officer Taylor, watch him. I'll be back." Then she storms off to the counter. She interrupts Leroy from taking the customer's order. He quickly walks off.

"Is all of this necessary?" Sherman questions.

"Mr. Ford, you're not in any trouble. She is just confirming you work here. I'm just back up."

Sherman shakes his head with a look of embarrassment. Ms. Fox is animated as she talks to the manager and frequently points in Sherman's direction. After 5 minutes, she walks over to Sherman and pulls a cup out of her jacket pocket. "Mr. Ford, I need a urine sample. Follow me to the bathroom."

Sherman lowers his eyes as he walks pass his supervisor and Leroy. She holds the bathroom door ajar as she watches him piss into the cup. She labels it after he hands it to her. "Thank you and congrats on the new job. See you next week at 11am. Don't forget to wash

your hands, you do work in a restaurant."
She says sarcastically before leaving the
restaurant with the officer.

Sherman presses his bald fist against the
wall and exhales deeply. Leroy appears
in the doorway. "She's an asshole but
don't let her get to you."

"She just completely treated me like I am
a bitch ass nigga. I wanted to knock her
the fuck out. I can't. I can't do this. She
disrespected me in every way possible.
They want us to get a job and then she
comes in here on some slave master shit
trying to get me fired." He sighs.

"Well, you're not fired. I'm use to their
attitudes. I don't know why they feel the
need to tell me of your criminal history.
It's like they want me to fire you. However, you and I are good. You just keep
doing your job and following her rules,"

the supervisor replies while standing beside Leroy.

Sherman is fighting back tears, "Thank you. I really appreciate that."

"Ok, my floors won't clean themselves. I'm the real boss in here," the supervisor says as they all laugh and Sherman goes back to work.

CHAPTER 36

Butch is seated behind the steering wheel of his parked car. He is parked in front of a stop sign, facing a middle school. All around him is rundown section 8 buildings. He looks at his watch and the time is 2:30pm. He turns up the radio and he sighs out of the window. Then he notices a blue metal sign with white letters above one of the doorways that reads: Do you want to make $45k - $100k a year? Criminal record isn't an issue. Learn to code for free. Your future awaits. Come inside to sign up.

"Excuse me, Miss." Butch shouts to a well- dressed woman who stepped out of the building to talk into her cellphone.

She looks towards him.

Butch points to the sign. "Is that program real?"

"Yes! You should sign up. We have a class that starts next week." She says with excitement as she gestures for him to come on over.

He smiles and exits his car.

CHAPTER 37

The late afternoon sun is beaming down as inmates exit school while others are hanging out on the compound. Charlie is sweeping the compound. Brace is being pushed up the compound from his unit by Jon Jon. Barbwire is stalking Suga. He is watching him and Nancy play basketball by themselves from his position on the side of the gym wall. They are prancing around, missing shots, bending over, doing cheers and giggling as they play.

Nancy tosses the ball at the rim but it misses and rolls over near Barbwire. He doesn't touch the ball. Suga signals Nancy that he is going to get the ball. He prances over to the ball, turns his back to Barbwire and bends over and grabs the ball.

Barbwire walks up and squeezes his butt. Suga spins around and shoves him hard in his chest. His back hits the corner of the wall and he moans in pain.

"Fuck wrong with you, Motherfucker. This ain't that kind of party, Bitch. You better get your mind right before I beat your ass! Ain't no free feels around here, Bitch." Suga yells.

Barbwire rubs his aching back as he notices men looking at him. He sees Aryans walking in his direction. "Nigger, I should beat your ass!" He screams!

"Ain't nothing holding you back but your own fear. Trust you don't want to take this lost. I will beat your ass in front of your boys, Bitch."

Barbwire looks around again at everyone coming toward them. He charges Suga at full speed. Suga side-steps and he tumbles onto the asphalt. Nancy giggles and steps off the court as Suga walks toward him. Barbwire flips over and pushes himself up into a fighting stance. Suga puts up his fist and dramatically bounces around in front of Barbwire.

Charlie makes his way over and sees some of the Aryan Brothers preparing to get involved. He also notices Nancy with his hand under his shirt and holding the handle of his shank. Charlie signals the other Aryans not to get in it.

Jon Jon is nearly running full speed to get Brace over to the commotion.

Barbwire hits Suga twice in the face. Suga stumbles backwards in a daze.

"Come on, Suga. You can beat this, Bitch. I got your back." Nancy screams hysterically.

Barbwire smiles. "Faggot."

The whites and the black stand opposite of each other, prepared to go to war but not looking aggressively at each other.

"I'm the same Faggot , Bitch, whose ass you just grabbed. I'ma fuck you up. You two pieced me, Bitch." Suga says in tears.

Barbwire steps forward and throws a punch that misses. Suga hit him twice, once to the ribs and the other on the chin. Barbwire drops to one knee. He leaps up, charges and tackles Suga. They roll over on the ground. Then he lands on top of Suga and begins to choke him. Nancy eases his shank out. Some of the Aryans see this movement and does the same. At that instant, the guards rush in and grab the fighting men. They started ordering the other inmates backwards. They handcuff the fighting men and more guards storm the area and they usher the men off of the compound.

CHAPTER 38

Jon Jon stops Brace in front of the Aryans passing out the trays near the food counter. Blue Eyes, a sick Rakeys, and Nancy are standing behind them. The Aryan gives them all a dark brown food tray. A group of Aryans are in the line behind Nancy. The kitchen is packed with inmates eating. Jon Jon stops Brace in front of Skip's serving station. There are two slots with chicken soup. One is covered and the other isn't. Skip uncovers the covered slot by placing the metal top over the one that was uncovered. He gives each one of them a serving of the soup. After Nancy receives his serving, he removes the cover and places it back over the one he was serving them from.

Blue Eyes and Nancy follow Brace, and Jon Jon walks in the direction of Charlie's table. The tables are long picnic style white tables. He is the only one seated at the table. Bear and other Aryans are seated at tables close to him. All of the tables are segregated by race. The whites are eating from light brown trays. Charlie smiles to them and gestures for them to sit. A sickly looking Black Smoke is watching from his table with Marc and Dre. Psycho, The Devil and Bear are watching. They comply and take a seat at Charlie's table. Everyone, even the guards and the Warden are now focused on them.

"Thank ya'll fo joining me fur lunch. I tell ya, I don't reckon me will be too long. I'm sure hoping we can prevent any further altercations."

Brace nods his head in agreement.

"But that Bitch grabbed her ass. That is unacceptable." Nancy shouts.

Brace hushes Nancy with a look.

"Naw he disputes that. However, for the sake of peace, I will accept your view of the situation." Charlie says.

"You have no choice, Honey. I was there." Nancy says with sarcasm.

Charlie looks at Brace for help. "Nancy, please. Let me handle this."

Nancy sighs, starts looking around and his leg starts rocking as he clenches the shank in his waist.

"That's what we want too." Brace replies.

Charlie smiles as he bites off a piece of his cornbread. "By golly. That made my day. You have my word, It's over on my end."

"Nancy..." Brace says looking at him.

"What?" Nancy says sucking his teeth with a look of irritation.

"It's over. I need you to be cool with that...Are you cool with it?" He says, sternly.

Nancy sighs even louder and sucks his teeth. He rolls his eyes at Brace. "I guess."

"What the fuck do you mean you guess?" Brace says with irritation.

"Boyyyyyyy, don't talk to me like that. You really don't know me." Nancy snaps back as he squeezes his shank tighter. Blue Eyes looks in his eyes and shakes his head.

Nancy sighs and makes his lips flicker with frustration.

"Would it be ok if I arrange for you to talk to your friend to see what he wants to do?" Charlie asks with sincerity.

"She." Nancy replies.

Brace looks around with a look that says, I don't believe this shit.

"Ok." Charlie replies.

"Well, if it's cool with her, it's cool with me." Nancy says, calmer.

"I'll set it up. My goal is to get them out of the hole today and we continue to live in peace."

Nancy smiles. "Ok."

"I'll go see if I can arrange for you to see...her now." Charlie says before signaling the Warden. The Warden gestures for Charlie to come to him. He gets up. As he walks toward the tables, he passes Black Smoke. Black Smoke smiles as he says, "Told you he with them. You know what I'm saying." He says licking his lips and rubbing his hands.

CHAPTER 39

Sherman is defeated. He is leaning against the wall near the front door. Ella opens the door in her bathrobe and stares at him with concern.

"Hey." He says without looking at her. Tears start trickling down his face.

She goes and hugs him. The tears of years of suppressed emotions pour out onto her shoulder. She rocks him and rubs the back of his head until he drops down to one knee. She sits on the porch, lies his head into her lap, and caresses his back with one hand.

He cries for two minutes before taking the same seat. He wipes his eyes and looks at her with a forced smile. She gives a comforting smirk. He grabs her hand. "I'm sorry. I love you. Never meant to hurt you but I did." He says slowly.

She caresses his eyebrow. "How did you hurt me?" She says comfortingly. His chin drops to his chest as the tears begin to pour again. She ushers his chin toward her. "Look at me." She says, softly. He hesitantly looks into her eyes. "You can do this. Be strong. I got you."

He whines. "I'm not. I'm not as strong as you think I am. I'm tired of pretending. I'm tired of hiding." He replies barely audible.

"The Sherman Ford I love is human. He makes mistakes but he faces whatever he has to face. He knows he's not perfect. He knows he loves his family and that his family loves him. He knows bravery has nothing to do with mistakes he had made against the ones he loves. He knows love can only heal love. Do you love me?" She whispers with compassion and sincerity. He nods his head that he does. "Show me with you." She replies.

He sighs. "I slept with Susan."

CHAPTER 40

Suga walks into the unit and places his belongings in his cell. Then he immediately goes and knocks on Nancy's door before opening it.

"Hey Girl!" Nancy squeals as they rock in each other's arms. "Girl-l-l! I was going to turn up if they didn't let you out!" He says, laughing.

"Girl, give me one of those knives. They say it's squashed but I will kill that Bitch if he says anything to me." Suga says, seriously.

"I got you. I got four in here." Nancy says as he walks toward his bunk.

Brace rolls up behind him. "Hey, Suga." He says staring at his butt. Suga sees his lustful   gaze. He forces a smile. "I was starting to really miss you."

Suga throws his palms in the air, "Please, Mr. Brace. Don't."

"I got you out. You owe." Brace says with a sinister grin.

"I owe you? "Suga says, frowning. "Yea." Brace says massaging his groin.

"Please leave me alone. I'm trying to be nice to your annoying ass. Now get away from me." Suga says.

"Damn, Baby; at least let me suck one of those pretty titties." He says.

Suga runs behind the wheelchair and rams him into the back wall. Brace screams in pure agony as the impact crushes his legs beneath his knees. Suga tosses him out of the chair and starts beating him with the wheelchair. The hits breaks his ribs, shoulder and cause gashes in his head. "I told you to stop trying to kill me!!! You nasty bitch!!" Suga screams in rage. Nancy runs out of the cell at the same time as Jon Jon runs in. Jon Jon knocks Suga out with one punch. Nancy returns and immediately starts stabbing him in his neck and upper-body. A sick Rakeys and Blue Eyes race down to the scene with their knives in their waist. They immediately see Nancy stabbing Jon Jon's lifeless body, lying in his smeared blood. Blue Eyes grabs Rakeys' arm as he whips out his knife. They hear the guards screaming as they race toward them.

"Nothing you can do. He gone. He gone." Blue Eyes says. "Come on so we won't get caught with these knives," he says before they run to their cells and the guards mace Nancy and Suga as he is waking up. They eventually are handcuffed and lead away.

Barbwire is a part of the medical team. He and another inmate in their hospital uniform are pulling the stretcher. Two other inmates come behind them with another stretcher. The area is flooded with guards of all ranks and the Warden. They moving Brace out and he is barely breathing when he grabs the handle of Blue Eyes' locked door. Blue Eyes is standing in the doorway.

"Blue, please don't let them hurt her." He says before they rush him off.

CHAPTER 41

Charlie briskly pushes his trash-can into the unit. He signals the Aryans. The Devil, Skip and thirty other Aryans gather around him. The other races of inmates get closer to each other and some go and grab their knives as they watch the Aryans.

Charlie is furious. "There are forty more niggers in the bullpen. Tonight they are going to lockdown until they can clear dem. There are too many fucking niggas and bosses on this com-pound. I'm tired of this shit. We shutting it down before lunch. Devil, burn them down in the hole. When they call for lockdown after he burns the hole, that's when ya attack the niggas in your work-place. Now if you can get'm and hide them without being seen, do it, especially those shot-callers. Devil, set it off at 10am.

Guards burst onto the tier. "Lockdown!! Lockdown!! Lockdown!!!

Prisoners scramble to their cells. There are about thirty officers with riot gear. After they lock everyone down, they let Charlie out to clean the blood in Blue Eyes' unit.

CHAPTER 42

Butch is double parked in front of Ella's house as Sherman and Loretta, in her school gear, walk onto the sidewalk. He signals Butch to wait a minute. Ella comes a few seconds behind them. She looks skeptically at the car but forces a smile when Butch waves at her. By the time she gets to her car, Loretta is comfortably in her father's arms before getting into the backseat. Ella kisses him goodbye before he walks to Butch's car. As he gets into the passenger seat, Ella drives by and blows the horn. Sherman shakes Butch and Simon's hand. "Whhh-hhhhat's all of this?" Butch says with excitement.

"I'm back home." Sherman says trying to keep a straight face but his smile surfaces and he giggles.

"Wow. That's great." Butch says as he drives off. His phone starts ringing. He doesn't answer his aunt's call.

"I need to find out why these people haven't sent me my social security card. It's been months." Sherman says.

"Man, don't try to change the subject. How you feel?" Butch says.

"Youngsta, you nosey as hell. We good. I told her the truth so I am back home. The only drawback I can't get none until I take an AIDS test."
"Woooow. That's some funny shit." Butch says, laughing.

"A van be in the grocery store lot by my school that takes AIDS tests. It should be there now." Simon says.

After they drop Simon off at school, Butch parks by the Know Your Status van.

Two women exit the van as they get out of the car. The older woman has wide eyes, huge smile and a fresh natural hairdo. She shakes the other woman's hand. The woman leaves extremely happy with her test results in hand. The woman with the wide eyes turns toward them. "Hey Fellas, I'm Sharon. Ya coming to see me?" Sharon says.

Sherman shakes her hand. "I am."

"Come on in. I need you to fill out a form. The test results only take twenty

minutes. You'll be out of here by 8:20."
Sharon says smiling reassuringly.

Sherman follows her into the van.
A couple minutes later, they both exit.
She looks at Butch. "Your turn." She
says smiling.

"I'm good." Butch replies as he looks at
his phone as his aunt calls.

"You might as well. You're waiting anyway. Nothing wrong with knowing. I
promise, it won't hurt. I'll even give you
a lollipop and a pen." She says laughing.

He hunches his shoulders and follows her in. He goes through the same
process as Sherman. Sherman's results
come back negative. Then Butch's turn
to go in and get his results. "Sit for me,
Baby. I need to take your blood and get it
tested." Sharon says calmly.

"Why? Whatcha got to do that for?" He says, consumed with fear.

"Your test came back positive for HIV. I just want to make sure we didn't get a false positive." She says reassuringly.

He leaps to his feet. "Shit. It has to be wrong. I just came home from prison and I only fucked my girl raw." He says frantically. "I know she ain't got shit. She be feeding me vitamins and shit." He says pulling the pill out of his pocket.

"Let me see that." Sharon says, sticking out her hand.

He hands it to her and she examines it.

"Baby, this is Truvada. Truvada is a pill you take to keep you from catching HIV."

CHAPTER 43

Black Smoke is extremely sick
and walking sickly into the medical unit
of the prison's hospital. A guard is walking a few paces behind him. An Aryan
Brother appears at the opposite end of
the hallway and flashes the Aryan Brotherhood sign. Black Smoke stands up with
a look of readiness for war as the guard
disappears into a room. The Aryan
Brother balls up his fist and picks up his
pace toward Black Smoke. Black Smoke
does the same.

Barbwire creeps up behind Black
Smoke throws a punch and cracks him
across the chin. He goes unconscious. As
they drag him into an empty examination
room, one of his shoes comes off. They
tie his hands behind his back and his feet

together with his shoestrings and hospital tape. They tape his mouth closed. He comes awake but is drowsy. The lay his upper-body across the middle of the examination table. His weak legs are half bent and his feet are touching the floor.

Barbwire pulls down Black Smoke's pants and boxers. They exposed his bare butt. Barbwire forces his penis inside of his rectum. Black Smoke tries to jerk his body to the side. The other man punches him in the face several times. He is tired. He is sick and he is weak. They rape and beat him repeatedly.

Then finally they lay the battered man across the examination table. His face is mixed with blood and tears. Barbwire smiles at him and kisses him on the chest.

Then he holds his finger over his lips. "If you try to scream, we will do all of this again." Barbwire says before ripping the tape off of his mouth.

"I'ma kill both of you. I swear." Black Smoke pleads.

"That's sort of hard to do after we whitewash you, Nigger. Have a drink with us." Barbwire says as he points to the other man. The man raises a gallon of bleach for Black Smoke to see. He looks away. Barbwire snatches his chin and holds it steady. Black Smoke holds his lips tight. With one hand, Barbwire pounds the man's stomach. His mouth opens in pain. Barbwire holds his mouth open by his cheeks as the man pours the bleach down his throat and nose until he convulses and dies. Then they begin to clean themselves   off but blood re-mains on their shirts. They exit the room at the same time that Marc and Dre enter the unit. They all pause. Black Smoke's friends spot his shoe on the floor and the blood on their shirts. They whip out their shanks and dash towards them. Barbwire sprints through the double doors down the other end of the hall. The other guy snatches his knife free. They surround him. Marc notices Black Smoke's lifeless body on the examination chair. He moves in. The man swings his knife but Marc stabs him in the neck and the blood squirts into the air and gushes out. Dre steps in and stabs the man thirteen times in the chest. Marc severs the man's head.

CHAPTER 44

Rakyes is doing pushups on the floor. Blue Eyes is laid back on his bed reading a book. A guard knocks on the plexiglass window. They both look toward him. "Mail." The guard said before sliding two envelopes under the door. Rakeys leans his face close to the plexiglass. "Are we coming off lockdown today?"

"If the doors open, you can come out," The guard says before walking off.

Rakeys picks up the mail and hands it to Blue Eyes. He immediately sits up on the bed. "Shit. This is from the courts." He is consumed with fear. "You read this." He says as he hands it to Rakeys.

"Oh wow. This is from the appeals court." Rakeys says with nervousness. Then he opens it.

"HOLD ON! Let me read this other letter first!" Blue Eyes burst out. "I want to ease into that shit." He says with a look of fear. "Sara? I don't know any Sara." He says more to himself as he opens and read it. It was a short letter. He holds up the two bathing suit pictures for Rakeys view. "This the white girl from the graduation!" He says, laughing.

"Whaaaaat? How she get your info?" Rakeys asks with a look of surprise as he examines the picture.

"When you're a pimp. All the hoes find you." He says jokingly.

"She nice. She's built like a white girl but she pretty. That white boy is going to killlllllll you." He says laughing. "When you write her back, get me a friend. I don't care if she fat, blind or live in a bubble. I want her." He says as they both laugh.

Blue Eyes snatches the picture back. "Now, read the letter." Blue Eyes doesn't blink as he watches him read the letter. "Slim, they granted your appeal. They fucking vacated your sentence! Wow." Rakeys says in total shock.

"What does that mean?" Blue Eyes says in confusion as he stoops on top of his bed.

"It fucking means you no longer have a life sentence! It fucking means if they don't retry you, you're going the fuck home!!"

Blue Eyes leaps up and his head slams into the ceiling. He grips his head and balls up on the bed in complete agony.

CHAPTER 45

Butch slams on the brakes, jumps out of the car and sprints pass the crowd of kids and adults in front of his building. The kids have on birthday party hats and a little boy has splattered pieces of food and liquids on his chin, bib and hands. He is smiling at his mother. The people look curiously at Butch who disappears into the building. He opens the apartment door and snatches the gun from his waist. He kicks the bedroom door open. Tonya jumps back from doing her hair in the mirror. She throws up her palms in fear. "No, Baby. Please don't. I'm sorry." She cries as she gets down on her knees. He towers over her with the gun aimed at her forehead. He is confused and furious. He slams the pill into her face.

"Bitch, how could you do this to me! I was good to you!" He says through clenched teeth. Tears start pouring down his face. "My life was already fucked up enough! You were the only good thing in it and you kill me?"

"I love you." She cries.

"Love me? What the fuck ya think love is? Everybody that fucking loves me hurts me. Pressures me. Ya don't know what the fuck love is! Ya selfish. Ya fucking selfish, Bitch." He presses the gun to her forehead.

She closes her eyes and clamps her hands together in prayer. "I was wrong, Baby. I was trying to protect you from catching it that's why I fed you the prevention pill everyday. I never wanted to hurt you. I didn't want to lose you. I love you. I'm sorry. I'm so, so sorry."

He takes a deep breath, closes his eyes and uncomfortably adjusts the gun in his palm. Instantly, the people outside started singing Happy Birthday loudly. He looks to the window and storms out of the house.

"Butchhhhhhhhhhhhhhhh, don'ttttttttttttttttttt leave." She pleads in desperation.

CHAPTER 46

Devil walks into lockup pushing a large plastic trashcan and carrying a container with a pump and short hose. The wheels on the trashcan squeak as he pushes it. Prisoners begin to peer through their narrow window. He parks the trashcan by the flight of stairs before he walks up them. Nancy is in the first cell. Devil stares into his eyes.

"Hey Girl, how can I help you?" Nancy says.

Devil squats and starts spraying the liquid on Nancy's ankle from under his door. Nancy jumps back and curses frantically. Devil continues to spray him and around the cell. Nancy runs up and starts kicking the door. "I'ma kill you, Bitch!" Nancy screams.

Devil stands and smiles at him before taking out a match book and holds it up before Nancy's eyes. Horror consumes Nancy. Devil strikes a match and slings it into the room before he starts peering through the window. Nancy tries to fan the flames on his ankles. He jumps on to the bed and the cover and sheet catch on fire.

Devil casually stops at each tier and cell with a black male inside and does the same thing. What he didn't notice as he set all of the cells on fire, Nancy and a majority of the others either jumped into the toilet or started splashing themselves with the water from the sink or both. Some yelled in complete agony as death succumbs them or rage. Marc along with several of the other prisoners begin yanking their cell doors open. Marc has a shank in his hand and he tries to pry the door further to slide out of it. Devil briskly exits the unit looking over his shoulders.

CHAPTER 47

Sherman is seated on the couch with Ella seated next to him with her head on his shoulder. Loretta is seated on his lap as they all watch TV. The only light in the house is coming from the TV and a glimpse from the street light. Sherman places his hand in Ella's. She kisses him on his shoulder and snuggles closer to him.

The TV show they are watching goes off. Ella kisses him on the shoulder again before standing and reaching for Loretta. "Bedtime. Let's brush those teeth and get in bed."

"Mommy, I already brushed my teeth." Loretta whines.

"When?" Ella says with disbelief.

"Daddy, told me to do it after we finished eating. See?" Loretta smiles.

"Nice job, but it is still bedtime." Ella responds

"Can Daddy read me a bedtime story?" Loretta says with excitement as she climbs off of him.

Ella looks at him. He sighs before slapping his hands on his knees. "Sure. I would love to. Lets go."

Loretta grabs his hand and leads him to her bed. She grabs his box from under the bed and climbs under her covers.

"Where you get that from?" He says with confusion.

"You left it on the porch. I took care of it for you, Daddy." She says

He kisses her on her forehead. "Thank you. You know I love you, right?" He says.

She nods her head. "And you know that I love you, Daddy. I got your back."

He moves the box behind him as he sits on the bed beside her. "Now where is that book?" He says.

"I don't want you to read me a book, Daddy. I want you to read me one of mommy's letters to you." She says.

"Ummmm. I have to see which one is appropriate for you to hear." He says as he grabs the box. When he opens it, he sees his social security card. "I have been waiting for this to come."

"Daddy, I keep everything that belongs to you. If you ever go to jail again, I will have a part of you with me allllllllllll the time."

He struggles to hold back a tear so he hugs her to hide it.

CHAPTER 48

Blue Eyes is packing his belongings into a laundry bag. After he completes his packing, he turns to Rakeys. He is leaning against the back wall. He extends his hand to him. Rakeys bypasses his hand and hugs him.

"I'm going to miss you, Youngsta, but I am proud of you. Proud of the man you have become. You still have an opportunity to create a beautiful life for yourself out there. I'm counting on you to make us look good."

"Thank you, Cuzzo. I mean, thank you, Sir." Blue Eyes says, sarcastically.

They both laugh as they separate and shake hands. "I am so thankful for you and this." He points to the bag. "If it wasn't for you, I wouldn't be going home...ever!"

"That's what real friends do. We help our brothers be greater. I support you. I always saw your greatness. Don't walk out of here and forget you're better than this place. You always have been. Make something of yourself out there."

"Will do, Cuzzo. I promise."

"Send me my money and tell Sherman, I'm still here. Get at me." Rakeys says.

"Time to go Marshall." The guard says from the door.

They shake hands again. Rakeys walks him to the door. "Officer, can I walk him out? I promise I won't run pass him out the door." Rakeys says half-jokingly.

"Prison on lockdown. Can't do it." The guard replies before shutting the door. Rakeys leans against the window and watches them as far as he could which is a few feet. Blue Eyes follows the guard onto the compound. It is 8pm.

The guard opens the door to the Control Area. He motions Blue Eyes to wait a moment as he steps into a room and closes the door. Blue Eyes looks around with interest because he has never been in the room. He hears movement behind him and turns around and sees Weirdo. He has a thirteen inch knife in his hand and hatred in his eyes. He tries to stab Blue Eyes, but Blue Eyes hits him on the top of his head with the bag. Weirdo stumbles. Blue Eyes is on him. He throws punch after punch after punch. The man drops the knife as he stumbles onto the wall. Blue Eyes scoops the knife up and repeatedly stabs Weirdo seventeen times from his head, neck and upper-body. Blood gushes out of the man's wounds. Blue Eyes pauses with a look of shock as Skip stabs him three times in the back. Blue Eyes dying body slumps to the ground.

CHAPTER 49

Butch drives recklessly through the night. He makes a sharp left turn and double parks in front of an apartment building to see Simon's mother cursing at him and tossing his clothes at him. He leaps out of the car as she is slinging a tennis shoe at the boy's head. Butch blocks the shoe as the boy shields his head.

"Ms. Barns, what's going on?" Butch says with a pleading tone as he holds his arms out to block anything else she throws. Butch notices all of the boy's clothes on the grass as if she tossed them out of the third floor window. People are standing around watching with disapproval or enjoyment.

"He think he's grown. But he ain't. He ain't shit! He not going to be disrespecting me in my house! I will beat that bitch ass. Fuck wrong with him!" She barks more at Simon than at Butch.

Butch looks at Simon who still has his arms over his head. "You disrespected her." Butch barks at him.

"Nooooo. I just told her I had to do my homework before I take out the trash. She went nuts after that." Simon says with tears in his eyes.

'Oh. Oh I went nuts. I'll show you nuts motherfucker!" She kicks off her shoes and makes a dash for him.

Butch grabs her and walks her backwards. "Ms. Barns, let me take him over my house until ya calm down. I'll take him to school and when you ready, I'll bring him home."

Butch says as Mailman Mitch pulls up and jumps out of the car.

"Butch, let her go." Mailman Mitch says, gently. Butch looks over at him. Then he releases her. Mailman Mitch smiles at her. "Knucklehead is acting up again in your house?" He says.

"Yes. You know his ass! And you know I will fuck him up out here." She barks back, calming down.

"Now, we don't need you going to jail over something stupid. Look, we going to straighten him out. Let him go with Butch and you and I can talk, ok?"

"Ok. Mitch, but he ain't taking none of his fucking clothes. As a matter of fact, take all those fucking clothes off! Get naked, Bitch!"

"Ma, I only have on a shirt that you purchased. Mr. Butch bought me everything else."

"Well, take of my damn shirt!" She screams.

Simon takes off the shirt and gently tosses it off to the side of her. That enrages her. She leaps for him, but Mailman Mitch grabs her and tells Butch to take him and leave. Butch is furious, but they ride in silence. Butch drops him off at his aunt's house before grabbing his guns and jumping back into the car. He races across town and parks in a middle-class community and walks across the street into the upper-class community. The streets are dimly lit. He disappears into the woods behind the mini mansions. He puts on his mask and whips out his guns. He peeps out at the houses as he looks for the one he is in search of. He finds it. He looks around and does not see anyone on the streets. He goes and rings the doorbell. After a few minutes, a man opens the door. Butch cracks him as hard as he could on his forehead with the butt of the gun. The man collapses. He drags him in the house, ties him up with phone cords and begins searching the downstairs area for people.

"Michael, who is that at the door." Quality shouts.

After hearing the voice, he continues to search the house until he was certain no one else was home. He walks into the door with the gun aimed at Quality, who is confined to a hospital styled bed.

"Oh God, no. We don't have anything here but take what you want. I won't give you any problems." Quality pleads.

Butch slowly removes the mask to reveal his face. "What's up, Yo?" Butch said sarcastically. Quality starts mumbling and is unable to put his words together. Butch searches around Quality's body and bed for a gun. Then he leans on the railing of the bed. "Where the money at?"

"Butch, ain't no money." Quality says in complete fear.

Butch punches him right in the center of his face with such force that it breaks his nose. "Don't be saying my damn name. Now, where is the money?"

"I'm broke. I had to pay $3 million for the death of my connects' people. I'm broke, yo. And I am fucking paralyzed from the waist down. You fucked me up, yo. We were going to get money together."

Butch slams the butt of the gun against Quality's leg with no reaction from Quality. "Look, Quality, I am in a serious bind. I need the money or I am going to kill you and your people. Where is the money? This is the last time I'ma ask you."

"I can't give you what I don't have. There is probably $1,000 in that top drawer over there but I am broke. Please, man, do what you have to do to me but my peoples don't have nothing to do with this."

Butch hunches his shoulders then takes the pillow below Quality's bed and smothers him to death. He retrieves the $1,000 from the drawer and Quality's Rolex. Then he leaves and notices E's house. He looks around the outside of the house and only sees a living room light on. He forces his way into the house from the patio door. He searches the house and only finds $6,000. He hears a car pulling up. He runs to the living room window and peeps out. He sees E's girl. He flees out of the back door.

CHAPTER 50

Ella is watching herself in the mirror as she takes her earrings out of her ears. She has on a white silk gown. Sherman walks up and rests his palms on her shoulders and inhales her scent at her neckline. She closes her eyes and smiles. He runs his hand up the sides of her hair and massages her scalp as he turns her toward him. The love and desire glows in their eyes. They kiss as he raises her gown over her head to reveal her purple bra and g-string against her dark smooth skin. She leans her head back and looks into his eyes.

"I love you so much."

"I love you and I promise to never leave you. You are everything I have ever wanted in this world. You make me happy. I love, being loved by you." He replies.

She wraps one hand around his neck, pulling him into her kisses and uses her other hand to pull his boxers down to his knees. She sits up on the dresser and uses her feet to push his boxers further down. Then she pulls him closer with the heel of her feet as she opens her legs. He takes his finger and holds her panties away from her pussy. She grips and strokes his manhood before scooting closer to him and inserting the head inside of her.

"Damn." He moans.

CHAPTER 51

Devil, Barbwire, Bear, Skip and Psycho are seated in a large waiting room not far from the Warden's office. Psycho glances up at the clock. It reads 12:15 am. He pushes himself up.

"Ya did good. I'm proud of ya. This is what true White Power looks like. Today we showed strength. We are the superior beings. White Power!" He shouts as he holds up the Nazi salute.

The others stand and follow suit and return to their seats.

"How many casualties do we have?" Psycho asks.

"Somewhere near fifteen but there are at least 100 injured. Those DC Blacks are warriors. Mean and durable niggers." Barbwire replies.

"I could have told you that. However, we could have minimized the casualties. I can't allow this to persist. When we go in here with the Warden, let me do all of the talking. We have to finish what we started at least with the real threats out of the DC Blacks. I'll let him know that this is in the best interest of the institution but more importantly in the best interest of us. Rakeys, Dre, Marc, Brace and anyone else ya feel should die, must die tonight. Those are our demands." He says confidently.

Charlie walks into the room and leans against the wall and puts his foot on it.

He runs his hand through his hair. He holds a balled-up wet paper towel in the other hand. He smiles at Psycho. "What is this? A church meeting?"

Psycho faces him with his hands on his waist. "No. I was telling them how we are going to move forward."

"Oh, it sounds like you're calling the shots now. That's pretty raw. Now I am not that smart. Some would say a dumb country boy, but I thought that was what I did?" He says sarcastically as he shakes his head.

Psycho briefly stares into the eyes of the other men. "I think we have way too many casualties. This operation was a huge failure. None of the threats were really eliminated."

"Huh? I see. But, what I am not clear on is are you offering me suggestions or are you running shit around here now?" Charlie says.

Psycho loosens his neck and takes two steps toward Charlie.

"Speak up? There are too many niggers and too many bosses on this here compound. Are ya a Boss, Psycho? Are you a shot-caller, Psycho? Uh, let me be mo clear. Are you the leader of the Aryan Brotherhood, Psycho?" Charlie says with this menacing look in his eyes.

"New leadership is needed. I am willing to do whatever it takes to restore control of our Brotherhood and this compound." Psycho.

"Ya know, it sounds like you have butter-flies shitting on your tongue because you ain't answering the fucking question. Cowards can't produce a coup. They only good for a clean lick on some balls." Charlie says casually. Then Charlie flings his hands downward like he had water on them but three of his fingers were pointing down. Immediately, Barbwire starts stabbing Bear in his neck. The others leap up, but are confused as to what they are supposed to do. So they look around at each other as the blood squirts all over the walls.

Instantly, Charlie flings the balled up paper towel into Psycho's face. As Psycho flinches, Charlie stabs him three times in the heart and once in the gut. He grabs Psycho's shirt and stares into his eyes as his eyes roll into the back of his head. Then he releases the corpse and it slams onto the floor.

Skip steps in and jams his icepick into Charlie's neck and twists it and yanks it upward. Charlie dies instantly. Skip releases the body and stares at the others as it crashes onto the floor.

CHAPTER 52

Butch looks depressed on the passenger seat of Mailman Mitch's car. He is just staring into the silence of the night through the front windshield.

"Ah Ya know. I think you're a good brother. I really do. And that boy loves you like you been in his life all of his life. Ya know. We need more brothers like you that have been caught up in that life. That's what these boys need, but I meet so many good brothers who don't believe they have anything to offer these youngins. They just don't know the fact that they changed is enough. Our boys want the real. They don't have to know what you did. They can look at you and tell in your eyes that you have been through something. They want men that can relate to them. They think they little

asses really been through something."
Mailman Mitch goes from serious to
laughing at his own jokes as he pets his
belly. He is in his mailman uniform.
Then he switches back to seriousness.
"But the men can't be straddling the
fence. Ya know. If they are, they're going
to do more harm than good to these kids.
Ya know. You represent that change is
possible. That's why I am going to ask
you, Butch...let the boy go because sooner or later he is going to see something
that is going to give him permission to be
like his cousin Yesterday. That's why he
gravitated toward you. He was expecting
you to be like his cousin. Then he saw
you were a genuine dude that accepts
him for who he is, but what's more important than that, is that you are taking
the time to be in his life. A man that he
can turn to. Ya know, a real man that is
guiding him and will put your proverbial
foot in his ass when he does some dumb

shit. I love you for that alone. I just know it's better for him, if you let him go, Butch. Thank you man for recognizing you had to do this on your own. That shows what kind of a man you are. I'll pull him in while you get yourself together. And I will continue to help you. You're a good brotha. Ya know. It makes you an even better brother because you called me and told me that you have one foot in these streets. I like you and I believe you are going to make it through this rough patch. I got you, My Brotha. Ya know."

Butch sighs. "Thanks. He's in there asleep. Let me figure out how to tell him. I'ma wait until he gets out of school so he won't cut up in class. Then I'll meet up with you around 6pm and hand him off."

"Yea. You do that. Ya know. That sucker is going to take it hard but I got'em." Mailman Mitch says before looking at his watch. "Butch, Man, I have to get to this job in twenty minutes. I'll call you around five to see how it's going."

CHAPTER 53

Sherman is at work seated across the table from Butch and Simon in one of the middle booths inside of the restaurant. Simon is using a straw to sip on his drink. He is seated against the wall and Butch is on the edge. A carryout bag is in front of Simon. He taps Butch on his shoulder. Butch frowns at him as he wipes crumbs off his red shirt that Simon just got on him. "Let me out. I'ma wait for you in the car." Simon says.

Butch lets him out. He goes and sits on the passenger seat of Butch's car parked directly in front of the restaurant. Then Butch pulls out an application and hands it to Sherman. "I'm getting ready to start this program. They're going to help me get an IT job starting at a minimum of

$35 an hour. I figured you could get with this. I'm sure it's more than you're making now."

"How you feeling? You look off." Sherman questions with concern.

"I have to work some stuff out. I'll holler at you later. I have to have a conversation with Simon. Let me get with him and I'll tell you everything after I make it through this conversation." Butch says with regret.

"Wussup?" Sherman asks

"I'll holler at you when you get off." Butch says as he stands. Sherman stands and they walk out of the restaurant. They stop in front of the door and talk for a few seconds. The car didn't attract their attention as it made a U-Turn from the other side of the street.

"Red shirt!" Old Face shouts from the passenger seat of the car after stopping next to Butch's car. Butch and Old Face lock eyes. A teenager walks up to the side of Butch and fires one shot into his head. Sherman sprints back into the store. The teenager stands above Butch's body and shoots him three more times in the head before running down the street as the car pulls off. Simon is staring in shock. He hops out of the car screaming with no sounds coming out of his mouth. He sprints toward Butch's dead body. Sherman steps out of the store and grabs him before he reaches the body. He buries and holds the boys head in his chest to prevent him from looking at his dead mentor. For a few seconds, he tries to scream but no sounds came out. Then finally his screams equals equaled his pain.

"I got you. I got you. I got you now." Sherman says…

THE END

These are the other 2 books in this series:

 **"THE HILL"** is a raw fictional tale that exposes the impact of hopelessness, distrust, and relationships formed based on need and power. THE HILL is a place where simple decisions can have deadly consequences.

Follow Sherman as he begins serving his prison sentence at Lorton Correctional Compound. This compound houses some of the deadliest men in the world. It's a penitentiary so dangerous that the other maximum-security prisoners don't want to go.

Sherman made some bad choices in his life. Now, he will either live or die from the consequences of his choices.

THE WALL is the sequel to THE HILL. it's a story about friendships, betrayals, family abandonment and predatory behavior. Real Gangsters have been known to scream behind...THE WALL. No one is safe. There are no leaders. Everyone is a killer.

Other works by Lamont Carey:

 **"Dead Before 18..."** is a navigational guide written to and for young boys who have and will face a complex world that demands making decisions

and promises consequences. It is written from the perspective and experiences of the writer; who made many mistakes while learning how to be a man.

The goal of the book is to make these boys and young men aware of the pitfalls, so they might avoid lives of self-destruction.

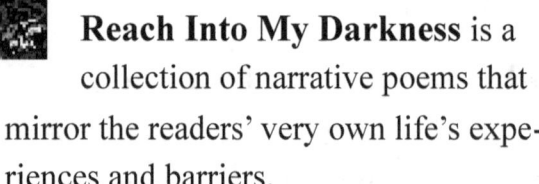 **Reach Into My Darkness** is a collection of narrative poems that mirror the readers' very own life's experiences and barriers.

The goal of the book is to inspire self-reflection, self-expression and empowerment.

 **Your Art Is Your Empire** is a guide for performing, recording, and spoken-word artists who want to turn their dreams into a business...and ultimately...an empire. The book covers such topics as: legal business structures, taxes, marketing, creating a bio, and creating their first product and more.

Imagine is Lamont Carey's award winning CD containing such hits as "I Can't Read", "Confidence", "I Hate This Place", "She Says She Loves Me", and ten other electrifying spoken word pieces. Digital files are available for sale on iTunes, CD Baby, amazon and more.

T-Shirts

Keep Your Hustle but Change Your Product. The difference between illegal and legal is the product. Order your T-shirt from the website and help spread the word!

A Creative Mind Is A Goldmine. Lamont believes artist have the ability to change the world and make a living off of their creations. No more starving artist! Order your T-shirt from the website! www.lacareyenterprises.-com/clothing

Lamont Carey is an international award- winning spoken word artist, filmmaker, playwright, actor and motivational speaker. For booking arrangements for speaking , workshops or performances for your group, students, prisoners, employees, conferences, or at any other event you are having worldwide, contact LaCarey Enterprises, LLC:

lacareyentertainment@yahoo.com

You may visit the website at:

www.lacareyentertainment.com

Send fan mail to:
LaCarey Entertainment, LLC P.O. Box 64256 Washington, DC 20029